Complete. Price Fourpence.

# DICK THE DIVER.

OR

## THE LONDON TREASURE SEEKER.

LONDON: T. ROBERTS, RED LION COURT, FLEET STREET.

# DICK THE DIVER:

OR,

## THE LONDON TREASURE-SEEKER.

LONDON:

T. ROBERTS, RED LION COURT, FLEET STREET.

# DICK THE DIVER.

WHAT DICK SAW ON THE RIVER.

# DICK THE DIVER.

## CHAPTER I.

### WHAT DICK SAW ON THE RIVER.

AT eleven o'clock on the night of the 7th of November, 1866, the American steamer *Valparaiso* dropped anchor in the Pool.

It had come up the Thames, drawn by a noisy little tug, through such a dense fog that even its red lights were scarcely distinguishable; and Captain Carter, as he went ashore and felt his feet on terra firma, was thankful he had escaped the many dangers of the river.

"I shall never forget this night," he said. "It's about the densest fog I've ever seen."

And he never *did* forget that night, though it was not the fog that reminded him.

As soon as the captain had left the ship, the crew began to make all comfortable for the night: the fires were reduced, the men turned into their berths, and only three persons were left on the deck.

Two of these were watchers, the other was a passenger.

The latter was a man about middle-age, somewhat stout, with a bronzed face which told of travel, and a merry expression which told of success and happiness.

He was dressed in a reefing jacket, blue trousers, and a glazed hat, and looked somewhat like the mate of a ship.

The other two men were common sailors, one a young fellow of five and twenty, the other about twenty years his senior, with black hair, a swarthy face nearly covered with beard, but eyes that seemed to pierce through you, and spoke of unmitigated and reckless villainy.

Both were watching the passenger, and as he paced to and fro on deck, their glances followed his every movement.

But he seemed perfectly innocent that he was the object of their attention.

Leaning over the bulwarks, and smoking his cigar, he tried to pierce through the darkness; but only a few dim lights were visible, and he heaved a sigh as he murmured—

"Well—well, this is a miserable night! I feel chilled already by the way old England has welcomed me. But never mind; when I left London ten years ago I hadn't a penny in the world, and now I come home rich, to meet those who loved me even in my misfortunes, and to make them happy at last."

The two men watched him now more narrowly; and as he bent over the vessel's edge in a deep reverie, the elder man spoke—spoke in a low, hoarse tone, which was an evidence of his treacherous purpose.

"Now, Ned," he said, "brace up your nerves—the time has come: one blow, and our fortunes are made; but that blow must be swift and sure. One cry, and we are lost!"

Unconsciously, the man smoked on—full of visions of a wretched past, and a future which was to atone for all: a parting scene which had stirred him up to the great struggle for fortune, and a welcome which was to repay him for years of hardship.

But never again was he to gaze upon the loved ones—never again would he be pressed to a faithful heart.

The church of St. Paul's tolled the hour of twelve: it was his death-knell!

Gliding like a serpent, the man whom the elder villain had called by the name of Ned crept up behind his victim; slowly and surely his arm was raised; the heavy life-preserver was poised one moment in the air, and then—whizz!—it descended upon the wretched traveller's head.

One groan—one suppressed groan of agony was all that escaped him, and he fell—not on the deck—but over the edge of the bulwarks, his hands dangling helplessly.

"Well done, mate," said the elder man, in a hoarse tone of approval. "Now, quick!—let's drop him over. Yet, stay, we'll see that his rhino is all safe."

The fog which had so enveloped the river now began slightly to lift, and the moon to struggle through the gloom; and so as they laid the body on the deck, with his ghastly face upturned towards the sky, they could see at once that he was dead.

The two villains might have been expected naturally to have robbed their victim, and flung him over into the water, whose swiftly running current would have wafted its ghastly burden to the ocean.

But they did nothing of the kind.

They drew from his pocket a waterproof case; opened it, saw that it contained bank notes and papers; and then closing it again, replaced it in its receptacle.

Then, tying a rope to his neck and another to his heels, they raised the body, and gently lowered it over the side of the vessel until it reached the water, where they allowed it to remain while they got ready a boat.

All this time, such had been the silent way in which the crime had been committed that the two murderers imagined themselves perfectly unobserved.

It was not so.

Just as the body of the traveller was being lowered, a little wherry containing a single figure had glided up under the shadow of the great steamer.

Its occupant was a boy about sixteen or seventeen years of age, dressed very poorly, and evidently one of the unfortunate class who pick up a living as best chance and good luck will permit them.

His intelligent, frank, and open countenance, however, was one which had only to be seen to be admired and trusted.

His bright eyes dilated with astonishment as he saw the body gently approaching the water; and steadying his boat under the ship's shadow, so that he could see without being seen, he watched the movements of the two ruffians.

"I'll follow these men," he thought. "There's a secret here, and I'll follow it out, or my name's not Dick the Diver!"

Had the boy belonged to any other class of society, he might at once have raised an alarm and called the police; but he had received in this world far more kicks than halfpence, and had a wholesome dread of the myrmidons of the law.

He preferred, consequently, depending on his own resources; and so when the two men had lifted the body into the boat, and began to row away, he followed as gently as he could.

The men did not proceed very far. Making their way towards a spot where a high breakwater of blackened timber was built out among the ooze and slime, they drew ashore, and taking the body with them, filled its pockets with heavy stones.

Then they fastened a rope to an old rusty ring, which was always nearly covered with water even at low tide, secured the other end to the neck of their victim, and once more rowed out with him into the stream.

Here, at some distance from the shore, they dropped him quietly into the river: they had, in fact, *anchored the dead body* with its wealth untouched, not to be made use of until all fear of discovery was over.

Quickly they rowed back towards the steamship now, and the lad at a considerable distance followed.

Up the sides of the *Valparaiso* they clambered: once more they paced the deck. The murder had been done, and none on board was the wiser.

But the boy had seen their doings, he had noted the name of the ship; and already in his mind a scheme of punishment and retribution was being planned, of which they little dreamed.

As soon as all was again quiet, the lad, who seemed to skim as easily over the dark river as if it had been broad daylight, turned his boat's end once more towards the spot where the assassins had placed the body.

Cautiously looking round him to see that no one was watching, he sprang on land, moored his boat, and began to haul ashore the ghastly receptacle of wealth.

Long and tedious was the task; and as the moon began now to throw its cold glitter over the river and the shore, the boy's heart thumped with dread.

What if he should be observed—what if he were seized in the very act of hauling ashore and searching a murdered man!

But all seemed quiet: not a sound was to be heard but the far-off buzz of the city, and the rippling of the water, and the unfrequent sighing of the wind among the rigging of some vessel. And so, with arms which ached in every muscle, the boy hauled away, until at length the calm, still face of the dead glided out from the dark stream.

One shudder—one momentary chill of dread as the pale-faced form rolled to his feet—and then the lad began his search.

Eagerly he sought in every pocket, until he at last found, pinned into the breast of the coat, the waterproof case, over whose contents the eyes of the murderers had glistened.

This, without even examining it, he placed in his pocket, and had just succeeded in doing so, when a dark object glided round the projecting wall.

The lad saw it and its occupants, and gave a low, gasping cry.

The Thames police were upon him!

## CHAPTER II.

### DADDY SPINDLE'S KITCHEN.

N a street in one of the lowest parts of Rotherhithe — a street which ran down steeply towards the river—there stood a house somewhat apart from the rest.

It had attained to the dignity of being detached from the fact that one of the houses adjoining it had been burned down and never been rebuilt, while the other had fallen down in a gale of wind, and left a hideous patch of waste ground on the edge of the stream.

The house which was thus left to itself was utterly uninhabitable in the upper storeys; its old, tottering walls were shored up, and part of its roof was off; but on the night of that 7th of November, 1866, a bright light streamed forth from the under-part of the building, and the sounds of laughter and loud conversation were to be heard even at the unseasonable hour of midnight.

Ever and anon along the dismal thoroughfare, lighted by murky lamps, a figure would be seen hurrying—sometimes an old man bent with age, sometimes a woman hugging a baby to her breast; and then again a lad or a young girl: but they all made their way to the portal of the dilapidated house.

At the door on the basement sat a woman in a box, whose face, round, red, and fat, was greasy with warmth, even on that chill night—for she was swathed in clothes like a mummy—while a tumbler of steaming grog stood on a little table before her.

On this table was also a kind of money box, with a slit in the top; and as each of the passengers passed in, two pennies were dropped into the receptacle.

Mother Spindle hardly ever took the trouble to receive the money herself: all comers seemed to know her: and dropping the coppers into the box, they mumbled a kind of frozen good night, and hurried into a large inner room, where there were rest, and light, and warmth.

Inside this room was a collection of all ages, and both sexes. It was, in fact, a huge kitchen, and crowded to excess with persons cooking, eating, and drinking.

Near the fire was an old man of peculiar appearance, who seemed to be one in authority.

He was possessed of a huge head, with shaggy gray hair, a large face of the shape of a full moon, a large hook nose, a wide, grinning mouth, while his body and his legs were so shrunken that he looked as if the whole of the substance of his frame had been crushed upwards to his brain.

He was as busy as a bee: cooking for one, helping another, keeping order with a long pewter spoon.

"Now, that soup, Daddy Spindle." "Come on, hurry up with that sausage," and so on from all corners came the cries of the motley gathering.

And who were these people? Were they thieves?—were they beggars?—or what?

It would be difficult to say. They were, in fact, of all classes; but in that room they were all on an equality, and Daddy Spindle asked no questions. All he required was that they should pay their rent and no more.

Presently, just as the hubbub of cries was somewhat stilled, and the hungry tramps had appeased their appetite somewhat, there was heard a sound of some one rushing at full speed along the silent street; and then, with a run, a figure flew past Mother Spindle, flinging his twopence into her lap, and nearly upsetting an old man sitting near the door.

It was Dick the Diver.

His face was very pale; his clothes—never good—were now torn in ribbons; his hands were torn, too, and bloodstained; and altogether he had the appearance of some one who had had a hard struggle for life.

"Why, what's the matter, Dick?" cried a big, burly lad about his own age, but whose face displayed at once the difference of his character. "Have you been diving, and met a shark? You look scared and knocked about enough."

"I did meet sharks," he said, "only they were the police. They found me diving after some treasure, and they spotted me. I clambered up the wall, got on top of the railings, and tore my clothes and hands; and if I hadn't led the way along Murphy's-alley, where they tumbled down the pit, I'd have been locked up."

"What are they after you for?" asked a voice; and turning round, Dick was confronted by a tall, pale youth, with ash-coloured hair, who had just entered in time to hear the last part of the conversation.

"Why?" asked Dick.

"Oh! it doesn't matter," returned the youth, quite calmly, as he removed a pipe from his mouth; "only they're searching the street now, and will be here in a minute."

"The Cage, Daddy Spindle—quick!" said Dick.

The old man seemed perfectly to understand the meaning of this mysterious term.

Passing to the side of the huge fireplace, he opened a cupboard-like door, and, hurrying through it, led the way down a steep staircase of brickwork—so old and dilapidated that it threatened almost at every step to throw them into the cellars below—from which, as they descended, there issued a smell like that from a sepulchre.

But both Daddy Spindle and his companion knew their way; and, making all haste, they passed through an open space in the old wall, where the plash of the river and the dripping of water could be distinctly heard.

Here, in a little cellar about six feet square, Daddy stuck a sputtering candle in the wall, and left Dick to his reflections.

He had scarcely re-entered the room before the police, reinforced now by four shore constables, entered the room, where a hundred curious eyes were directed at them, and fifty hearts beat high with that inexplicable fear which the poor and wretched feel in the presence of the representatives of the law.

The police took a hurried glance round the kitchen; but among the quiet groups which were gazing furtively at them, they could see no one to resemble the form of him who had darted so impetuously away from them just before.

"Who are you a-looking for?—'cos he aint here," said the youth with the ashen hair, addressing the inspector.

"Be careful, Master Bob," said that worthy, severely. "I am looking for one who has murdered a man, and has been robbing his body. We caught him in the act, and saw him examining the bank notes. They'll all be stopped at the bank; so be sure, any of you, if you take a bribe, you'll be discovered. Now, if any one of you knows anything—"

"We don't," rang out a chorus of voices. "There's no one down here as indulges in murders."

"We saw the man enter here," said the policeman.

"Well, if so," said Daddy Spindle, putting his arms akimbo, "perhaps you'll be good enough to search the place, or say which is the willain, as my lodgers here is werry tired, and want to go to sleep."

A hurried consultation took place between the police; and seeing the hopelessness of a search in such a place, they turned to go.

"There'll be a reward," began the inspector; but he said no more, for there was an unmistakable sound of hissing; and so, determined to watch the place night and day, they departed, leaving all present in a state of terrible excitement.

Dick the Diver had come in for "a good thing," *that* they one and all agreed; but not for an instant did they entertain the idea of murder.

Dick's occupation was a hazardous one; but they were quite assured that, search as he might for treasure on the bodies of the dead, or elsewhere, he would never hasten any poor creature from the world, were he to have the chance of a thousand pounds.

Many a time, when he had plunged into a fire in search of "treasure trove," he had thrown away all chance of booty for the sake of rescuing some child from the flames; and his name of Dick the Diver was as well earned by his saving of human life as by his diggings in the mud, or his diving after lost property.

But bank notes had been mentioned, and the mouths of all present watered.

"Bring him up," said more than one crowding about Daddy Spindle. "He must share among his pals."

The old man assented at once.

"Yes, yes," he said; "remain quietly here, for the police are artful, and may return. I'll go down to him."

Once more he passed through the secret opening by the large fireplace, and made his way to the spot where Dick the Diver was sitting.

He glided along so noiselessly, that the young lad observed him not; and so the old fellow surprised him as he sat in the centre of the Cage, examining a piece of paper.

The waterproof case had been secreted, but on his lap lay a crisp bank note.

The old man's eyes glistened as he poked his huge, unseemly head in at the open door.

"They're gone," he said.

The boy started and clutched his treasure.

"What're gone?" he cried—for, immersed in the reading of the paper, he had forgotten all.

"The police," said Daddy Spindle, in an unctuous voice. "I got rid of 'em for you. I soon put them to the rightabouts. But there's worse coming," he added, in a low voice—"yes, worse coming. The boys upstairs have heard of your luck, and they're wanting shares."

"Shares!—why, they don't know what I've got," cried Dick. "Whatever it is, it doesn't belong to me."

"Ah! they won't wait to think of that," cried old Daddy, with a knowing leer; "they'll get angry if you refuse—of that you may be sure. But, I tell you what, if you'll give me that bank note, I'll say you've bolted."

"But they'll search the place," said Dick.

"I'll get you out," returned Daddy, whose fingers were already itching and clutching at the prospect of coming wealth. "Give me the money, and—"

The boy suddenly seized him by the arm.

"Daddy," he cried, excitedly, "the time's come now—the time when you said you'd tell me my name if I paid you well. I've waited and waited, and now I *will* pay well. Here is a ten-pound note: it is yours if you'll tell me all."

The change that suddenly came over the old man's face at these words was something awful.

To say that he turned pale would fail to express the matter in the slightest: he became of a greeny shade; his eyes, always goggled, now seemed to start from his head; his mouth dropped, and he stood there for an instant in the light of the sputtering candle, like some hideous apparition from the other world.

"Why, what is the matter?" asked Dick, in alarm. "Is there anything so horrible in my asking my name?"

The old man, by a great effort, pulled himself together, as the saying is.

"Why, no," he said, stammering: "but don't ask me now—don't remind me. I can't yet say anything. I don't want ten pounds. I'd rather be without it if that's the price."

The boy still grasped his arm, but more tightly than ever.

"The day may come when I'll force it from you," he said. "But, meanwhile, tell me only my name—only my name: I'll ask no more."

"And you'll swear not to reveal who told you?"

"I will—I do."

"And you'll give me the money?"

"Yes—yes, I will."

The old man bent down and whispered in a low tone, as if he were afraid the walls or the plashing waters might tell—

"Dick Ashton! And now, then, give me the money, and let me go. Listen: they are getting impatient, and are thumping on the wall. Pull that grating—that's it. You had better stay away all night, and return to-morrow."

The boy still hesitated.

"Here's the ten-pound note," he said; "but here's another—here are two—if you'll tell me all you know of the past. I long to know about my mother—my father—"

The old man uttered a low, gasping cry, and raising his hands aloft, fled away in the darkness.

"There has been some foul play—I am sure of that," he murmured as he blew out the light, and crept through the grating out on to the waste land; "or why should he feel such terror at the mere mention of them? By heavens! I will discover it—no matter what comes of it, I *will*."

Hurrying now across the dark space, he made his way into a narrow and unfrequented alley which led into the more busy part of Rotherhithe.

It might be imagined that, after the excitement of the night, Dick the Diver would have gone to rest.

But no.

The various late lodging-houses which he passed were not even glanced at; and though the clock struck two, he pressed on until he reached a rather narrow street by the river.

Here he paused before a little house, built somewhat after the style of a country cottage, though now, begrimed as it was by the smoke of the dense district, it was difficult to tell what its original colour was.

Late as was the hour, a light burned in a room on the basement, and at the window of this Dick knocked gently.

Some one within at once pulled aside the white curtain, and seeing who it was, said, in a low voice—

"Come in."

Without hesitation, Dick approached the door, lifted a latch, entered a dark passage, and made his way into the room.

---

## CHAPTER III.

### GENTLEMAN MORRIS.

THE scene into which Dick was now introduced was one which was as utterly different to the one he had just left as could well be imagined.

It was a little room, not more than ten or twelve feet square, where the spirit of cleanliness seemed to reign triumphant.

The furniture—scanty, rickety, and seemingly almost useless—could not, with its cracks and flaws, conceal the fact that all was neat and tidy; and the patched and worn linen of the bed that stood in one corner was a still further evidence of the fact.

On this bed lay a man asleep—a man with long hair which, flowing over the pillow, was almost as snowy as the linen—a man whose well-cut features were now shown up sharp and angular by the ravages of a dread disease.

By the fire sat a young girl about sixteen, whose coarse costume, patched and threadbare, could not conceal the loveliness of her form, and whose beautiful face, in a setting of golden hair, beamed out like a flower in a rugged wilderness.

She smiled and held out her hand to Dick as he entered; but the tears sprang to her eyes as she pointed to the bed.

"He is going—going fast," she whispered. "I fear there is no hope."

"Don't say that, Miriam," he said, as he sat down beside her. "I've brought that which will cheer him up, put new life into him, and restore him to health more than all the doctors in the world. See here."

He drew out two bank notes, and showed them to her.

The girl's eyes glistened as she looked at them, but she shook her head slowly.

"I am afraid it is too late," she said, "you will say so too, when you speak to him. His mind has been wandering all day, and he talks of the old times, which are such a blank to me now. Hark! he wakes."

They turned towards the bed, and saw that the old man was moving restlessly; and heard him mumbling in his half-unconsciousness.

"Ah!" he murmured, "they'll never buy baskets of Gentleman Morris any more. Gentleman Morris is going where there are no distinctions of persons. Ah! Dick, I see you, though all is very misty. Come close, lad, and let me take your hand."

Dick the Diver approached, and, sitting on the edge of the bed, took the old man's thin palm in his.

"I bring you good news, sir," he said. "I have money here in plenty. See, here are two five-pound notes; they will buy you comforts, and we shall soon see you well again."

A weary smile overspread the old man's face; but he shook his head sadly.

"Good lad, good lad!" he said. "I thank you from my heart; but it is of no use. The die is cast. I am going to leave this world; and when I am gone no one will miss me but Miriam and you. She is clever; she will live by basket work. And then, if you will give her a little money, she will be able to get a few things and go on comfortably. But never—never do I wish her to seek out her friends; better be poor—aye, far better —than be with them."

These words, which were said with strange fervour, were utterly unintelligible to Dick, and partly so to Miriam.

He had arrived in Rotherhithe about a year before, and he and his daughter had earned their living at basket-making; but such was his style and behaviour, and kindness to all—even in his great poverty—that he had obtained and preserved the title of Gentleman Morris.

Miriam herself knew nothing of whence they had come in her childhood, or who were her friends; all she could tell was that they had lived a wandering life, and that the constant terror which haunted the mind of her father was that they should fall in with her friends.

More he had refused to say; but throughout their wanderings he had ever been kind and indulgent.

"I shall be alone in the world," said Miriam, sadly, "when you are gone, dear father. Do not talk of it—do not let such a thought prey upon your mind. Dick has brought money to get you comforts, and by the spring we will be always happy together."

The old man smiled.

"Well, well, children—dream on till the last," he said. "Leave me now—I will sleep again."

"Can I go out in the shed?" said Dick to Miriam, when he had bidden Gentleman Morris good night.

"Yes, Dick—no one is there. Here is a light."

He took it, pressed her little hand, and went along the dark passage into a shed at the back, where, on a heap of straw, he composed himself; and soon, in spite of his adventures, in spite of his treasure, in spite of the scene he had just left, tired Nature asserted herself, and he slept soundly.

He was awakened by some one shaking him by the shoulder.

He started up, and saw a pale, sorrowful face bending over him—the face of little Miriam.

"Dick, come in—he's gone!" she murmured, in choking accents. "I fell into a sleep, and I was awakened by one shrill cry. I started up, and saw him gesticulating violently and trying to speak; but ere I could reach him he was dead."

With a sorrowful heart, Dick the Diver made his way to the room where the old man lay in the still majesty of death.

The young girl here burst into an agony of grief.

"Dick," she cried, "how utterly wretched and alone I am! I know no one but you. Father, even at the last moment, would not relent; and where my friends are I cannot even dream. How can I live here in constant dread?"

"Why are you in dread?" asked Dick.

"Nearly four years ago a man, dark and evil-looking, called upon my father when we were living at Gravesend."

"'Why are you living in this poverty,' he asked, 'when you might be living in wealth?'

"'I like poverty,' said my father, with a smile, 'anything better than *their* money.'

"'But the child,' pursued the man—'let the girl come with me, and you shall have two hundred pounds.'

"I shuddered, and slunk up to my father's side.

"'Never!' he cried. 'Leave my house, Robert Oldfield, and never enter it again.'

"The man scowled, and went away; and until six months ago I never saw him again; for my father had fled from Gravesend that very night, and he had found it difficult to track us.

"He came into this very room, and seeing me, he praised my beauty, as he called it, and renewed his offer; but my father grew so enraged that he went away, with a hideous scowl, saying—

" 'Very well, Gentleman Morris, very well. I'll return no more until the grave has closed over you; and then I'll *have* her, as sure as I stand here!'

"Now," added Miriam, with a shudder—"now you understand my dread?"

"Yes," said Dick, musingly, "but I will protect you; and who knows that we may find these friends of which you speak. Has your father any papers?"

"Yes, many; but he would never let me see them."

"We will look at them, then, when your father is buried," he said. "And now I will go out and get you something, and see about the funeral. We must say we found the money in the room, or we shall not be able to account for it. I wouldn't say I picked it out of the river."

"And did you—all that money?" she asked, eagerly.

"Yes," said Dick, with a smile—"that and much more. Do not look so hard at me, I didn't steal it."

And then he hurried away.

Preparations were duly made; the body placed in the coffin, and placed in an empty room; and while Dick the Diver slept in the shed, Miriam remained in the little parlour.

The funeral day came at length. Gentleman Morris was placed in his last home; and Dick, returning to the house after the ceremony, found Miriam with the blinds down, and trembling with dread, with her face white, and her eyes glaring wildly.

"What is the matter?" asked Dick the Diver, as he instinctively shut the door.

"He has been here," she said, shudderingly. "He peered with his evil eyes through the window, and tried to enter the room. But I shrieked aloud, and knocked on the floor, and the landlady came up. I heard him tell her he was a friend of my father's, and Mrs. Wood advised me to see him. But I refused, and pleaded so, that she said—'well, then, open the door, and tell him what you mean. I will protect you.'

"I opened the door and confronted him.

" 'Miriam,' he said, trying to assume a kind voice—though I could see he was bursting with passion—'I am here to take you to your friends. You have too long been kept from them. No more poverty, no more wretchedness and hard work. Will you come?'

"There was only a struggle in my heart.

"Should I go? No! If this man was one of the friends against whom my father had warned me, then I thanked him from my heart; and if nothing else warned me, the man's baleful, eager eyes would have done so.

" 'No, no,' I said, 'I will not go. I will remain here and work, as I have done before. I never wish to see you again.'

" 'Very well,' he said, with a scowl; and went.

"But I must leave here at once, Dick. I know what he will do—he will bring others to take me by force."

"Yes, you must leave this place," said Dick. "But where are these papers of your father's?—they may tell us much."

It was not long before a batch of papers, yellow with age, was lying on the table before them.

Many of them were nothing but old letters, which told much of the past, but nothing to guide them in the present. But at length a strange look came over the face of Dick the Diver.

He turned pale and then red with excitement.

"Miriam," he said, "I think I have solved the mystery. We will leave here to-night."

"And you will take me to my friends?" said the young girl, clasping his hand, and looking wistfully into his face.

"Yes, we will go together," said Dick. It is a long way, but that is no matter. We have money, and can go by train. Then we shall have to walk five miles across country. But we'd better go at night to avoid him."

"Yes, yes!" said Miriam, eagerly, and with tears in her eyes. "Dear, dear Dick, I have indeed found a friend at last. But you do not tell me where we are going, or who are my friends."

"We are going to Durford, about thirty miles; and then on to Selburne Abbey," said Dick. "But don't ask me any more. I don't want to disappoint you; and if I haven't solved the mystery, it won't do for you to think me foolish, and romantic, and so on. If we don't find them, we'll return to London, and hide away from your enemy. We shall give him the slip better by going to the country, even if we don't do any more good."

That night—leaving a week's rent on the table of the little parlour—the boy and the girl glided out into the darkness, without being observed by any.

## CHAPTER IV.

### THE SCENE AT THE CROSS ROADS.

S Miriam and Dick the Diver made their way along the narrow and murky thoroughfare, many an anxious glance did she cast around her; but not a soul appeared to

rouse her fears, and the railway station was reached in safety.

Both Dick and Miriam were dressed in mourning, and no one took any notice of them on their journey.

The train rattled into Durford Station; and Miriam, with a light heart, found herself plodding along the dark road which led to Selburne Abbey.

Dick the Diver was the first one to rouse her to a sense of danger.

"I do not know your enemy," he said; "so if you see any one near us, watch him closely."

The very idea of being followed by her hated persecutor, after their successful escape, made the girl shudder.

"Yes," she said, "I'll keep strict watch."

They went on rapidly, until, reaching a little ale-house, Dick went in to seek refreshment, leaving Miriam outside in the dark shadow of the inn, where she could not well be observed.

He had not been there five minutes before he came out again with the necessary food and drink; but in that five minutes something had occurred to change the happy, hopeful girl into a trembling, shuddering figure, leaning against the wall for support.

"Why, what ails you, dear Miriam?" he cried.

"There—there!" she cried, in a faint, weary voice; "see there, at yonder table sits my enemy. He has tracked us after all!"

Dick looked, and as the light of the inn lamp fell on the man's face, his heart stood still with terror.

There, flushed and scowling, even over his drink, sat the elder one of those who had lowered the body of the murdered man over the bulwarks of the *Valparaiso*.

For an instant, Dick the Diver—gazing upon the villainous face of the man as he sat beneath the inn lamp—was unable to decide what to do.

At present, of course, the murderer of the unknown traveller knew nothing of him; but to Miriam he was the impersonation of terror.

Clutching Dick with her trembling hand, and looking up into his face, she said, in a low voice, as if afraid that the slightest whisper would reach her enemy—

"Oh, take me away, Dick!—anywhere, anywhere! Back to London even, if you cannot think of any spot elsewhere."

"Hush, Miriam," said Dick, "there is no occasion for that. Be guided by me, and all will go well. Creep behind that barn yonder, and eat and drink something—you must be faint. Then we'll get through yonder hedge, and make our way along the fields until we are safe from him."

The girl obeyed mechanically.

Indeed, her horror of the man had for the time taken from her all power of action or even volition.

She ate her humble meal in silence, and then waited in patient dread while Dick went back to the inn, gave back the articles he had brought out, and took one more glance at the villain whom he already looked upon as their common enemy.

Then they made their way through the hedge, and hurried along under its protection for a long distance.

The night was very still; and they felt, when they had proceeded about a mile and a half, that they had certainly eluded pursuit.

At the cross roads, therefore, where they had to turn to make their way to Selburne Abbey, they once more trusted themselves to the high road; and, after glancing at the sign-post, were just about to hurry on once more, when a dark figure sprang from a hedge and confronted them.

"Hallo!" cried a well-known voice, "I've got you at last."

The words were, of course, addressed to Miriam, who, white with terror, clung to Dick for protection.

"What do you want with us?" asked Dick the Diver, boldly. "We are not interfering with you; so let us go on our way in peace."

"I'm not interfering with you, my young fellow," returned the man, "so you can go on as soon as you like. I should be sorry to deprive your friends at Selburne Abbey of the pleasure of seeing you. Ha! that's a home thrust, young shaver. So clear out, the girl goes with *me*."

And ere he could be prevented he grasped her wrist.

For an instant Dick measured the fellow's height with his eye, to see what chance he would have in a personal encounter.

But the man, besides being broad and powerfully built, was possessed of a large bludgeon; and so soon as reasoning could give him time to think, he said, as calmly as he could—

"Are you not making a mistake? This young lady can be no acquaintance of yours, and it is easy to see that she does not wish to have anything to say to you."

The man swore a loud oath.

"Be off with you," he cried, "or you'll find it the worse for you. This young lady, as you call her—Miriam, daughter of Gentleman Morris, basket-maker—is going with me to her friends—to those who love her, to those who will care for her."

"In that case," said Dick, "we had better all go to Selburne Abbey together."

The man burst into a loud laugh.

"She's not going to Selburne Abbey," he said. "But she's going to her friends, and with me. So be off. Come, Miriam, you have no one to dispute with me now—come."

And he tried to drag her away.

"Villain!" cried Dick, "you are wrong here. She has a protector, and one who would lay down his life for her. Leave her, or you will find the truth of my words."

The man laughed savagely.

"Why, you pigmy, be off, or I'll brain you with this cudgel!" he shouted, as he raised his stout stick aloft.

"I know you are good at murder," said Dick, eyeing him steadily, and pointing in the direction of London. "Do you remember the night of the 7th November, when you lowered your victim from the deck of the *Valparaiso*?"

The man, still holding his cudgel aloft, started back with a yell of rage and fear.

"You young villain! You imp of the devil!" he cried—"you shall die for this."

And releasing his hold on Miriam's wrist, he sprang forward.

But Dick was prepared for him.

Unused in his encounters, which were always with boys of his own size, to use any other weapons than his own fists, he had forgotten a purchase he had made that very morning.

Now, however, he placed his hand in his breast; and, in an instant, the bright barrel of a revolver shone in the moonlight.

"Back, or I fire!" he cried. "A murderer's life is nothing to take."

The man saw that he was foiled.

The girl had fled away along the road; and he saw by the stern resolution of the boy's face that he was not to be trifled with.

He lowered his bludgeon.

"You have foiled me this time, you whelp," he cried; "but you've laid up a bad store for yourself. I'll have my revenge, mark me; and a terrible revenge it shall be."

And with these words, and muttering horrid imprecations to himself, he turned and hurried away.

For an instant, Dick the Diver glanced round him in trepidation.

Where was Miriam? Could she have gone the wrong way, and run the risk of again falling into the hands of the villain?

But no, his dread was of short duration.

Out from the shadow of the hedge came hurrying a little figure, dressed in white.

"Oh! let us hurry on," she cried. "I shall never, never be at rest until we are beyond the reach of that wretch."

"Fear not," said Dick, "we are safe from him for the night; he will not venture to follow us now that he has once seen my pistol. What makes me fear is the future. What

can *he* know about Selburne Abbey? What friends *can* he mean, if they are not those I am seeking?"

Miriam did not answer.

She seemed lost to everything but the necessity of hurrying away; and clinging to her companion's arm, she pressed forward as if fatigue was utterly unknown to her.

Go on, you two young lives, press forward to the goal you seek!

Alas! if ye did but know to what you are hurrying, you would turn back, and fly even to the poverty and wretchedness of London, rather than face the unknown sea of danger.

Another mile brought them to the confines of Selburne Abbey; and here, as soon as the lights of an inn just about to close came in view, they pulled up, and engaged rooms for the night.

They had scarcely done so, and retired to rest, when another traveller arrived and hired a room likewise.

This was none other than the enemy of Miriam Morris.

## CHAPTER V.

### DESOLATION.

N spite of the lateness of the season, the next morning rose bright and beautiful; and as Miriam and Dick, after partaking of a good breakfast, made their way to the summit of Selburne-hill, the young girl clasped her hands in pleasure.

To her—imprisoned as she had been in that wretched place in Rotherhithe for a whole year—the mere gazing at such a scene was happiness intense.

Far away, as far as the eye could reach, stretched the undulating country, bright and lovely in the light of the morning sun, with a stream threading its silver way through green fields edged by nodding trees.

White cottages, and red-tiled farmhouses, and ivied turrets of churches, pleasant gardens and grassy knolls, valleys and gentle hills—all quiet and beautiful beneath the deep blue sky. Such was the scene that Miriam gazed on.

"I should like to stop here, and never, never leave it," said she, as she leaned on Dick's arm.

He knew not why at the time, but a pang shot through his heart as she spoke these words.

He understood it well not long after.

"It is, indeed, a beautiful place," he said; "I should not mind it for a home. See yonder house, with the white front, with that fanciful tower, and that mass of greenery around it."

"Yes," cried Miriam, clasping her hands; "oh, what a beautiful place! Is that where we are going?"

Dick the Diver laughed.

"We must not be too hasty," he said. "I have not yet discovered whether my idea of this mystery is right. Let us hope it is, for *your* sake. Come, let us hurry on—right across these lovely fields is the way—at least, so the landlord of the Lion in Chains told me."

They went on hurriedly now; until at length they reached, through green meadows and over bubbling brooks, the outskirts of what was known as Selburne Lodge.

It was a pretty place, not more than two storeys high, for the house was built out over a large space; and round its brickwork-pointed gables the tall poplars nodded, and the flower gardens spread—deserted now by the blossoms, but still trim and green.

At the thickset hedge which skirted it, Dick paused.

"Remain here for a little while, Miriam," he said; "I will go in and see if I am on the right scent."

So saying, he pushed the gate open, and, entering boldly, rang the bell of the inner door.

A pompous servant in livery answered the summons.

Had Dick been attired in the costume which he wore at Daddy Spindle's, it is more than probable that Thomas would have threatened him with the dog.

As it was, the lad's bright face, coupled with his genteel dress, won the flunkey's respect, and he said politely—

"What is it you require?"

"I wish to see Mrs. Ashton," said Dick.

"Mrs. Ashton, eh? leastwise she's not Mrs. Ashton now, she's Mrs. Henry Dashwood. What name shall I say?"

"Richard Ashton."

The man's eyes opened, and his jaw dropped, in profound astonishment.

"Master Richard Ashton!" he repeated. "Why, not the son of—but there, it's no matter of mine. Come in; the mistress will see you at once, I know."

The man was right.

Not a moment elapsed before he was ushered into the presence of Mrs. Dashwood.

He had expected to see a woman of middle age, of genteel appearance—a person of naturally well-to-do appearance, living in such a home.

He was quite unprepared, consequently, for the sight which was presented to him.

A woman of some forty years, with so much of beauty left in her face that she seemed many years younger, though the lines of care and sorrow had settled here and there, and her cheeks had begun to hollow with decay.

She smiled as he entered the well-appointed room, and pointed to a chair, saying—

"Sit down, my lad. And pray what Ashton family do you come from?"

"That is what I want to find out," said Dick, boldly, but respectfully. "I don't know yet who was my father or my mother; but I come here on other business, madam. Here are some letters which, I believe, belong to you."

He handed her some of the papers which he had found in the waterproof case of the murdered man, and then seated himself to watch the result.

Mrs. Dashwood seized them eagerly, and turned pale as she saw the writing.

"These were written by my first husband, poor fellow!" she said. "He was drowned eight years ago in the *Brighton* steampacket on his voyage to Chili. Yes, yes—these letters are his; and here are some of mine. How strange! How did you get possessed of these?"

"You say your husband was drowned, madam," said Dick. "Was his name Mark Ashton?"

"Yes."

"And was he branded on the chest with the letters 'M. A.'?"

"Yes, yes—he was."

"Then," said Dick—little calculating, in his enthusiasm, what might be the effect of his words—"then Mark Ashton, your husband, was murdered on the night of the 7th of this November, on the river Thames, as he was coming home to you."

Mrs. Dashwood sprang from her chair, and stood gazing at Dick for a moment, her eyes glaring, her bosom heaving, her whole form shuddering with emotion.

Then she sank down again into her chair, white and weary, murmuring—

"Mark returning to me, and murdered! It cannot be. Tell me all, child, tell me all!"

Briefly but boldly Dick the Diver told his story—the murder, the lowering of the body, the mooring it in the river, his examination of it, the finding of the money, the police chase, and, finally, the use to which he had put some of the money for Miriam and himself.

The lady, as he spoke, was overwhelmed with grief; indeed, the violence of her grief was such that Dick was often alarmed.

When he had finished speaking, she drew him to the window, saying—

"And where is this Miriam?"

"She is waiting in the lane."

"And you—how do you know your name is Ashton?" she asked.

"I was told by an old man with whom I have lived since my childhood, whose hideous face has been the only one with which I have been familiar—Daddy Spindle."

Mrs. Dashwood shuddered, and looked intently and earnestly into Dick's eyes, murmuring to herself as she did so—

"So like—so like, and yet I dare not think it!"

"I must speak to my husband," she said, suddenly; and ringing the bell, she sank once more into her chair, motioning Dick to resume his.

When the servant had been despatched to Mr. Dashwood's room, he was not long in coming.

He was a man to whom Dick at once took an instinctive dislike.

Younger by some years than his wife, he had yet the wrinkles and seams of passion and debauchery, and had such a strange resemblance to the murderer of Mark Ashton that Dick glanced at him in astonishment.

"Is anything the matter?" said Mr. Dashwood, somewhat angrily, "that I should be called away so suddenly from Mr. Hunter?"

"You can put off your champagne and cards for half an hour, I should imagine, Edward," she answered, mildly—"especially when I tell you that I have this moment received news which may imperil your own position as master of this house."

He grew white with anger.

"How dare you speak thus before strangers, madam?" he cried. "Are our affairs of such a cheap kind that they are to be talked about by every strange boy you like to make a confidant of?"

Mrs. Dashwood rose and beckoned him to the bow window.

"Your rage is immaterial here," she said. "Come here, and I will tell you the story. There is the messenger, and *his* name is Richard Ashton."

"An impostor, of course," he said, with a sneer, as he sauntered after her.

Quietly Mrs. Dashwood told the story which had been narrated to her by Dick the Diver.

He listened impatiently, tapping the floor with his foot, and when Mrs. Dashwood had finished speaking, he said, with a supercilious raising of the eyebrows—

"And pray what do you think of this person's story?"

"Simply, I believe it," said Mrs. Dashwood, resolutely. "And I believe that boy, Richard Ashton, who sits yonder, is—"

He seized her wrist, holding it tightly, and glaring into her face.

"Hush! are you mad?" he cried. "Do you want to make all your children illegitimate, to cast shame upon us all, to make your own name a byword and a jeer? If you believe this boy, well and good. Mark Ashton is dead, and he cannot come here to claim you."

"But this boy, he may be—"

"Nothing but a clever young impostor," interrupted Mr. Dashwood. "He has simply read the letters, and thought it an excellent thing to represent himself as the person whom you name."

"Harry," said Mrs. Dashwood, pleadingly, "there is nothing in the letters which could suggest to him the truth."

"Why, hang it, madam!" exclaimed he, angrily, "it seems to me that you are anxious to brazen forth your shame, to disgrace your children, to ruin all of us. Let me see to this. I will go to this den of infamy which you speak of, and see what the old man means. Meanwhile, you spoke of a girl, Miriam Morris—the daughter of your sister?"

"Yes—she is even now waiting without."

The man's eyes glistened at this.

"She is a different person," said Dashwood. "I am only too glad to think that she is found. The boy must be rewarded for that, and we must keep her here. You will know her, of course, at once."

"Oh, yes!" said Mrs. Dashwood, with a weary sadness, as if her heart were exploring days gone by.

"Meanwhile," continued he, "I will take this lad into my study, and question him. Where are the papers and bank notes?"

"Here they are," said Mrs. Dashwood, and handed them to him, while he, with a sinister smile, turned to Dick, saying—

"My lad, follow me."

Dick the Diver had heard high words, and knew that he was the subject of an altercation.

He felt strange qualms at his heart; though looking out upon the pleasant gardens and the meads beyond, he thought how beautiful life would be there—there with Miriam.

He started from some such reverie—in which London and its great river were cast aside for ever—when Mr. Dashwood bade him follow; and with a wistful look at Mrs. Dashwood, and a chilling sensation over him, he went into the study.

Mr. Dashwood locked the door, pointed to a seat, and sat himself down opposite to him, saying—

"Now then, my lad, repeat to me this story that you have been telling my wife. I have no doubt you are well drilled in it, and can do so without difficulty."

Dick the Diver flushed crimson.

"I am not in the habit of telling falsehoods," he said; "and if you disbelieve me, it is useless speaking."

"I do not disbelieve you entirely," said the other. "Proceed, I will listen attentively."

Minutely Dick recapitulated the story as he had told it to the lady—Dashwood leaning on the table with both his arms, and looking into his face searchingly.

The man listened carefully, and when the lad had finished he leaned back in his chair.

"Well, this is a strange story, my lad," he said; "why didn't you give the alarm when you saw the body lowered?"

"Because the police wouldn't have believed me," replied Dick, boldly, though his cheeks crimsoned. "I have only been a poor boy all my life, and poverty's a crime in London. They could have got rid of the body long before the alarm was heard; and if not, I should perhaps have been sworn to as the murderer by the assassins themselves."

"You reason cleverly, my lad," replied Dashwood; "but, nevertheless, I don't believe you. You acknowledge to having robbed the body, but as to his being marked with 'M. A.' on his chest, and so on, I think it is simply nonsense. You've invented that because it's spoken of in the letters. This was simply some common sailor who fell overboard, and was bringing money and letters, with an account, doubtless, of Mark Ashton's death. I can readily understand why you are afraid of the police. However, go now and fetch the young girl, and introduce her to Mrs. Dashwood. Then I will speak to you again, and arrange how to dispose of you. She, of course, can remain here; but you must return to London."

Dick rose with a dizzy head, and staggered away to where Miriam was.

He found her with flushed cheeks and brightly eager eyes.

"Oh, Dick," she cried, "what a lovely place this is! I have been watching the children playing in the sun under the bright sky, and I longed to be one of them. Oh, how happy I should be if I had such a home, and thought I should never, never go back to that horrid London any more!"

Dick felt a choking sensation in his breast; but he was brave and resolute.

"Miriam," he said, "the people in there are your relations, and they wish you to stay with them. The lady is your mother's sister. I am to return to London, to seek my way in life alone; but you can stay and be happy."

The young girl took no notice of the sorrowful tone in which these words were uttered.

She clapped her hands with delight.

"Oh, how happy I shall be!" she cried. Oh! I can hardly believe it; and you, Dick,

you won't mind it, will you? You can come and see me; and then, you know, of course you couldn't stop here, because they are not your friends. And, besides, you want to be in London, don't you, to get on in the world? Oh, how happy I feel, Dick! You good, darling boy to bring me here!"

"Come," said Dick, quietly, "they are waiting for you."

If he had hoped that she would have said "I will stop, if you stop," he was wrong—bitterly wrong; and dizzy in his brain, and choking at his heart, he went his way.

He brought her into the room where Mr. and Mrs. Dashwood were awaiting her; he heard them say something about her being very beautiful; and then he was roused thoroughly from his dream by the voice of Mr. Dashwood.

"Will you walk this way?" he said, in a stern, resolute tone. "I want to show you another part of the premises."

Dick followed mechanically, and, to his surprise, found that Mr. Dashwood was conducting him to a side entrance, which led into a bye-lane.

Arrived here, he opened the gate, and stopped.

"Here," he said, giving into Dick's hands twenty sovereigns, "here is money, better for you to spend than your notes. I give you this in consideration of your having restored to my wife her long-lost niece. As for yourself and your other story, however, I believe you to be an artful, designing little thief, and that you only brought her here to obtain a reward. There is the road to London—take it as quickly as you please; and understand that if ever I find you lurking about these premises, I shall either set my dogs on you, or give you over to the police. You know what will be said about your keeping this precious story all this time and not giving information at once. Remember, I shall have no mercy."

And with these words he closed the gate and locked it.

Dick the Diver had been so utterly aghast that he was unable to answer a word, and when he saw Mr. Dashwood walking hurriedly off, he was for an instant utterly paralyzed by anger, hopelessness, and grief.

Prostrated by the idea of thus losing Miriam, and the home he had pictured to himself, he was entirely unable for a moment to speak; but at length, rousing himself, he cried in his loudest voice—leaning over the railing—

"Unmanly coward!—I shall be even with you yet."

Henry Dashwood heard the voice and the words, and remembered them years after.

It was useless remaining any longer; and

DICK TAKES A HEADER.

so, with a heart full to bursting, Dick the Diver turned his face towards London—alone as before.

As before!

More alone, more hopeless, more wretched than he had ever been in the gloomiest hour of his life.

## CHAPTER VI.

### A DIVE WITH A VENGEANCE.

DICK the Diver proceeded slowly on his way for some distance, when he came to a sudden stand-still, and sat down upon a fallen tree.

"Go to London, I will not," he said. "Why should I be frightened? Why should I be driven away thus? I will remain. I will find means of seeing Miriam—by heavens, I will!—and chance whatever danger there may be. She would never stop with them were she to know how I have been treated."

He remained and rested awhile, and then proceeded on to the Lion in Chains for refreshment. He knew well that any attempt on that day would be useless, and he determined therefore to bide his time.

See her he would, and ascertain if she was a consenting party to the arrangement which had sent him forth a wanderer and an outcast.

For this reason he kept the money which had been doled out to him by Henry Dashwood; in his own heart he believed it to be his own, and there was no shame in using it for his own purposes.

All that day he wandered about the precincts of Selburne Lodge.

Again and again he passed away from it in different directions, to gaze upon the beauties of the country side.

But in vain.

Ever and again his steps would bring him back to the one spot where lived now the only being he loved—with a friend and a deadly enemy he was well assured.

Night fell at last, however; and he had once more to seek rest at the Lion in Chains.

Tired out as he was by the events of the day, he slept soundly; but his dreams were still of Miriam, and Henry Dashwood, and the murderer and his victim; and he awoke in the morning unrefreshed and excited.

After partaking of a hasty breakfast he strolled away once more in the direction of Selburne Lodge, resolving to watch near at hand all day, until he saw Miriam enter the grounds, and then to see her and speak to her once more.

Hour upon hour passed, and at length mid-day came, but still no Miriam appeared;

and yet, such was his courage, such his love, such his resolution, that he lay there, still under the shadow of the hedge, watching and waiting, basking in the sunlight, as if Miriam was all the world, and he had but to wait for her coming and live.

He was rudely disturbed from his dream.

He had just caught sight of a fluttering black dress, and had approached nearer still, when a hand was laid upon his shoulder, and, starting up, he found himself confronted by three constables and Henry Dashwood.

The face of the latter was pale and determined.

"I give this fellow in charge," he said, "for loitering about with intent to commit a felony. Take him away. I will assume all responsibility, and will follow you in a few minutes."

Dick the Diver eyed him proudly, though his heart sank within him.

"Mr. Dashwood," he said, "you know that you are not telling the truth. I am no thief, and—"

"Prove it in court," cried Dashwood. "Away with him, my men; and I will be up at the court in half an hour."

As Mr. Henry Dashwood happened to be one of the county magistrates, it never occurred to them to dispute this most illegal proceeding; and accordingly Dick was seized by the collar and marched away along the road.

Now, it must not be imagined for one moment that our hero had the remotest idea of allowing himself to be captured in this manner.

He had resolved, in fact, on the instant, to make good his escape.

The first thing to be done was to take stock of the constables; and accordingly, walking quietly along, he glanced from one to the other of the three men whom Henry Dashwood deemed it necessary to employ to capture a small boy.

The one was tall and small-boned, like a herring, with a long and prominent nose, and sunken cheeks and lanky hair.

The second was a sturdy sort of rustic, with red locks and a fat face, and a nose like a piece of putty stuck in a lump of beef.

The third was as fat as a porpoise, with an immense paunch, which his belt seemed uncomfortably to compress; short waddly legs, a huge red face, and a head round as a bullet, and with not much more hair on it.

"Good," thought Dick—"these are all of the timid kind. I will frighten them, and then take to my heels and run."

Gradually sliding his hand into his breast pocket, he drew out his pistol.

Then, suddenly, he raised his pistol and fired twice in succession.

The effect was instantaneous.

The man who held him by the collar, who happened to be the one with the huge stomach, loosed his grasp at once; the other two stumbled over one another, and fell in the ditch; and without an instant's delay our hero bounded off like a hare from the hounds.

In the first of his calculations he was correct.

It took the constables some time to ascertain whether there was any one killed or wounded.

The lean man and the podgy rustic stared at each other inanely, while the fat man turned and turned in the vain endeavour to walk round himself in search of injuries.

But at length all were agreed that no damage had been done, and that for the honour of the force they must pursue.

So, gathering up their skirts, they commenced the chase.

They had seen which direction the fugitive had taken, which was by a path directly through the wood, towards the railway canal; and knowing that this would effectually bar the passage, they pressed on manfully.

It was a very rough route—in the forest the trees had fallen in many places, and the gnarled roots of others spread across the path.

Over these the police constables went stumbling and rolling, every now and then lumbering upon some spot where a treacherous patch of green concealed some deep hole full of mud and slime.

By the time they caught sight of the boy, they were in such a deplorable state that their ire was roused tenfold.

For pretty objects they looked.

The fat man, having rolled over more than his comrades, had dipped one leg nearly up to the thigh in liquid mud; while having been compelled to save himself as best he could, one arm was in just as bad a state.

But this piebald appearance was not the worst of it.

His hat was partially caved in, and his lumpy nose, having been bashed against a root, was bleeding all over his beard, and down his uniform. One of the others had torn the back skirts of his coat, which, as he sped along, flew out behind him like the tail of a kite.

The constable with the pasty face was now purple with exertion, and the great beads of perspiration were dripping from his forehead.

But still on they flew.

Dick the Diver, not knowing his way, was of course under a great disadvantage, having to pause every now and then to see where he was going, and soon, therefore, he heard the cries of his pursuers close behind him.

At length, to his dismay, he saw before him the glistening waters of a broad canal.

Here was a dilemma!

Not that Dick was at all afraid of the water; but if he took to his favourite element he would, of course, spoil all his new clothes, and he had not time to remove them.

Suddenly, however, a thought struck him.

Near the edge of the canal was a wide-spreading pine, one of whose branches extended a great distance over the water.

Into this, just as he had turned the corner, Dick scrambled, and was just enabled to hide himself amongst the dense foliage when the three constables, puffing and blowing, came to a dead standstill on the edge of the river.

The three men looked at one another.

"Where's the boy?" asked the tall one with the big nose.

"I don't know," said the fat man, who happened to be the sergeant. "Disperse yourselves up and down the bank, and look for him—I will wait here and see if he comes by."

And with these words he sat down, puffing and blowing, on the sloping bank.

"If we catches the boy," said the man with the pasty face, solemnly—"I appeals to you, sergeant, if three such hobjects as we are can go into any court with the prisoner. We shall be locked up for being drunk and disorderly, and spoiling our uniforms."

The sergeant tried to look majestic.

But it was in vain.

The three men looked at one another, and burst into a roar of laughter.

"Never mind," said the sergeant, "do your duty, and never mind the clothes. We can put it all on to the boy, and swear he wanted to murder us. Be quick, or else he will give us the slip."

Meanwhile, Dick the Diver had not been idle.

While the three discomfited bobbies were consulting below the tree, he had quietly divested himself of his coat, waistcoat, and hat, and strapped them on his back.

He waited only until the pasty constable and the man with the long nose had disappeared, and then suddenly, while the fat sergeant was wiping the blood off his face, he shouted—

"Hallo, old fellow, where are we now?"

And then, with a long dive, he rushed over the constable's head, and went plump into the canal, sending the water spurting into the unfortunate man's face, and nearly blinding him.

Before he could recover himself, the young hero of the Thames had swum across and stood dripping on the other side.

The fat sergeant jumped up, and sprang his rattle.

"Help, murder, help!" he cried, "the boy has escaped."

## CHAPTER VII.

### DICK'S FLIGHT—THE ROBBERY.

ICK THE DIVER heard the words of the fat policeman as he staggered to his feet and shouted, but still he stopped while he put on his waistcoat and coat.

Then he waved his hand to the constable; cried out, "Good-bye, my friend;" and amid the shouts of boys and girls, he sped away.

He had not the slightest conception of the route he was taking.

All he knew was that he was making his way out of the clutches of his enemies.

On he flew, directing his course as best he could towards a wide, open space which looked like a heath, with here and there cottages and brick-kilns dotted about.

He was unaware of the excellent start he had.

The truth was that there was no bridge anywhere near the spot where the constables had been so discomfited; and it was some time before the long man and his short man, who had, as the fat one said, "dispersed themselves," collected their scattered forces, and got as far as the highway.

When at last they did, they were utterly at a loss what to do.

However, the fat man solved the difficulty.

Seizing a little boy by the ear, as policemen always do, he cried, in a voice of tremendous authority, which came from the deepest depths of his huge stomach—

"Answer me, now, or you'll know the reason why. Where's that boy? Which way did he go? I saw you a larfing. Take care!"

The boy was pulling up his mouth on the off-side, as if he was trying to extract his ear from the constable's grasp by sheer tension of the muscles; but, awed by the presence of the three minions of the law, he bawled out—

"Boo-oo! Don't hurt me. Oh! please, sir, don't pull any harder. He went up that way, sir, along the lane towards the heath."

The fat man released his hold of the boy, and turned towards his comrades—his mouth compressed, his eyes wide open, and his eyebrows raised.

"I have it," he said, "that boy's given me an idea. That varment's gone to the lime-kilns to hide. We'll borrow neighbour Goslin's cart yonder, and follow him. He won't suspect we're in it."

A bargain was quickly struck with the rustic possessor of the old market-cart; and the three policemen, huddling themselves at the bottom of it out of the way, were soon trundling along the lane.

Meanwhile, Dick the Diver, tired with his long race, and overwhelmed by the event of the day, sought out a place of refuge.

For a long time he was unable to do so.

But at length an idea struck him, and a novel one it was.

Standing near at hand was a huge heap of bricks, ready for carting away.

Rapidly he clambered to the top, dragging with him four or five pieces of wood, and then he commenced making a hole large enough for him to crouch down in, scattering the bricks round him in such a manner that they should not attract notice.

Then he proceeded to roof himself in, placing the sticks across, and the bricks over them.

This was done very loosely, of course, but in such a manner that no one standing up on the edge of the pile could detect any difference in its rugged surface.

He resolved to remain here, as well as he could guess, an hour, and then make his way slowly across country to the nearest railway station, whence he could start for London.

For a long time he heard nothing save the feet of unfrequent passers on the road; but at length he heard the rumbling of a heavy cart, first in the distance, then coming nearer, then stopping near the brick pile.

Then the well-known voice of the fat constable was heard saying—

"I believe he's hidden somewhere hereabout, from what that boy we met said. Ugh! how that cart has jolted me. Let's get down and search."

To say that Dick's heart did not beat wildly now would be wrong.

It did.

It was, of course, a very serious matter for him to be caught now, after the way he had treated the police; so he sat still, and crouched up, listening.

He heard their feet as they stumbled about the rugged ground, and presently he heard a voice near him say—

"He's not up here, that's certain. He's given us the slip, and we'd better go back and make the best of it."

It was the voice of the long policeman.

"We shall be laughed at," said the fat man.

"We shall at any rate," replied the other.

"But I feel certain he's hereabouts," said the sergeant. "Let me remain here, and do you go for more men, so that we can scour the country everywhere."

There was some demur to this, but at length he heard the two men go off again in the cart, and the voice of the sergeant below the brick-pile, saying—

"I don't care one fig about that boy--not one fig--he can go to Jericho for me. Now I'll have my rum. I feel quite in a tremble after my exertions and that wetting."

Now was Dick's time.

Crawling down the other side of the pile, he cautiously filled one of the old pails full of dirty water out of the pools near, and then silently reascended.

It took him not a minute to crawl across to the side where the fat sergeant had now settled himself down upon a heap of bricks.

Quickly Dick took aim.

Then, just as the rum bottle was being raised with unctuous slowness to the fat man's lips, half a brick came plump on the bottle, dashing it from his hand, and spilling its contents over the ground.

"Ah, you varmint, I have you now," cried the enraged constable, looking up, and beginning to scramble to his feet.

But he had not truly spoken.

In an instant an avalanche of dirty water descended, blinding and nearly choking him; and, ere he had recovered sufficiently to give vent to his execrations, Dick the Diver had descended, and was dashing away along the road.

The constable attempted no pursuit.

"If ever I catch him again," he began to say, but he didn't finish the sentence.

Such a coincidence was utterly unlikely; so, in spite of his absurd appearance, he hastened to the nearest roadside inn, where he consoled himself over a large glass of rum, and in narrating a story of how he had been attacked by four footpads, and narrowly escaped with life.

Meanwhile, Dick the Diver, fearing now no interruption, hurried away across the fields, until he reached a roadside inn.

Here he inquired his way, and finding that he was ten miles from any station—having come completely out of his route—he resolved to remain for the night in the neighbourhood.

The place seemed quiet, and not much frequented; and so, as the day was now beginning to wane—it being the middle of November—he engaged a bed.

There was not much fear of pursuit now.

He felt quite certain, in fact, that Henry Dashwood wished rather to scare him away from the neighbourhood, and frighten him into never showing his face again, than to court an inquiry in a public court, which might lead to more inquiry than would be pleasant to himself.

So when he retired that night to bed, in a little room near the roof of the old inn, he never dreamed of anything but peaceful security.

The events of the day, however, so preyed upon his mind, that his dreams were anything but reassuring.

The evil face of the man who had murdered the traveller on board the *Valparaiso*, loomed out from a perfect haze of faces and scenes.

Again, with Miriam, he was treading the dark road; again the form of their enemy was following them in the gloom; again the parting took place at Ashton Lodge; again he was running for his life.

And running—he awoke!

Was it fancy?

The moon was shining through the window of his chamber, lighting it up with a broad belt of silver.

And there in the window, framed like a picture, was the face of the murderer!

Dick sprang out of bed, stumbling in his sleepiness over a chair, and rushed to the window.

But no one was there.

The moonbeams and starbeams had it all to themselves, lying everywhere in broad patches on the roofs and the trees behind the building.

Dick rubbed his eyes, and looked again.

Still nothing.

"Well," he said, "in London I'm not used to a soft bed, so I suppose I've been having queer dreams. That roof isn't much. I've climbed many a worse place than that. But then, they'd think me mad here, so I won't chance it. I suppose I've been dreaming, that's all."

So he went to bed again after seeing to the fastenings of the window, and placing a couple of heavy chairs against the door.

The hours sped on.

He dreamed again.

This time they were pleasanter visions: of Miriam, of old happy days, when, though poor and ragged, he had sat and listened to her singing over her work, and to Gentleman Morris as he told wild and wonderful stories.

And so morning came at last and Dick awoke.

Springing out of bed, inclined to laugh at his fears, he saw what palsied for a moment his senses.

There, on the chair beside the bed, where he had placed his clothes, was a heap of rags similar to those he had worn before he had found his treasure in the Thames.

He glanced round everywhere.

But it was too true.

The clothes were gone; and on the table was a little packet containing money evidently.

He opened it with trembling hands and a faint heart.

Inside it was a half-sovereign and these words—

*"I leave you enough to pay your lodging and take you to London. You are no worse off than of old. So cheer up and find more treasure."*

These cruelly insulting words were written in a hand which was utterly strange to him.

He fairly trembled with an agony of grief.

Miriam lost: his little store gone that would have helped him to leave his old wretched life, and rise in the world for her!

But he would not give up.

Passing down, he told his story, which was not believed, but set down to some impostor's trick; paid his score, and went to London weary in body and mind, arriving on the second evening.

The first sight he there saw showed him how the clouds of his destiny were gathering over him.

Making his way to Daddy Spindle's, he saw in the street a gentleman and a boy in close converse.

"What," he cried, "Bob Priall in that guise, talking to my enemy! Some other dread conspiracy is on foot. I must be on the watch."

---

## CHAPTER VIII.

### BOB PRIALL—A CURIOUS COINCIDENCE.

A FASHIONABLY dressed gentleman, mounted upon a beautiful bay horse, was cantering along Newgate-street one bright afternoon about a week after Dick Ashton's visit to Ashton Lodge.

A double eyeglass hung mysteriously on his nose, and through this fast-fop fashionable appendage he kept regarding the industrious pedestrians with a kind of quiet scorn.

A ragged urchin, about fourteen, without a shoe to his foot or a cap on his head, had been for some time dodging between the cabs, carts, and omnibuses, in order to keep up with the gentleman on horseback, whom he evidently looked upon as a customer for a chance copper.

For every now and then, when an opportunity offered, he got in front of the horse's head, and pulling a lock of his curly hair, looked up into the rider's face with a cunning, comical expression, exclaiming—

"Hold your horse, sir, if you please, sir?"

The double eyeglassed equestrian seemed to enjoy the efforts of the lad to keep up to him, and would slacken the pace of his horse ever and anon as if going to stop.

The little fellow's face would then brighten up at the thought of the penny shortly to be pressed into the palm of his hand.

Seeing the effect this style of acting had upon his ragged attendant, the gentleman continued it for some time, viewing it apparently as a rare sport, and thinking to tire the boy out.

In the latter notion he was mistaken, for the boy was not to be baulked.

He evidently divined the rider's intention, and kept a little in the background, until the gentleman, after a sharp canter, suddenly pulled up at the door of the Magpie and Stump—famed in the song of "My Lord Tom Noddy."

Darting now from behind a cab, the boy, much to the astonishment of the equestrian, who thought he had given him the slip, stood at the horse's head, with his expectant-penny-smile upon his face, pulling away at his curly lock of hair, and exclaiming—

"Hold your horse, sir—please, sir?"

The rider appeared annoyed at the boy's persistency, and said, sharply—

"Run away—run away."

"I've run away already, sir, to see your horse don't run away. Fine animal, sir—free action, noble chest. Take the bridle?—yes, sir, all right, sir."

"It will be all wrong, if you don't step it."

"If I don't take the bridle from you? Yes, sir, here I am."

And, suiting the action to the word, with a profound stage bow, he stretched forth his hand.

"London assurance is triumphant," said the gentleman, laughing. "Here, take the bridle, and mind you watch him carefully."

With these words the gentleman leisurely sauntered into the tavern, where he had appointed to meet a few sporting men to complete some bets upon the approaching Derby.

Having arranged this business, he asked some of them to give him their opinion upon the horse he had just purchased, and which was standing outside.

For this purpose two or three of them emerged from the tavern, and were loud in their praises of the animal.

Suddenly Mr. Robert Lamont, a friend of the equestrian's, caught sight of the boy who was holding the bridle, and burst into a loud laugh.

"By all that's difficult in cashing an accommodation bill!" he cried, "behold, my friends, the new tiger that Harry has 'bought' on the strength of the good fortune he has spoken of."

"Good," cried the gentleman, after he had joined in the laugh of his friends, "a good idea. Come here, young anti-soap and superfine, and let's hear what you can do."

"Stand on my head, sir, and play Jim Crow on the soles of my feet, climb a greasy pole, turn over head and heels from London to Greenwich, roll down the hill, clear starch and iron ladies' caps, ride a hoss, clean a hoss and sleep on his back, sir; row a—"

"Stop—stop, these are numerous accomplishments truly," cried the gentleman; "but say, would you like to be a tiger?"

"And go and perform at Hashley's? Oh! wouldn't I rather!" he replied, with a grimace of delight.

"No, I don't mean that," replied the gentleman, laughing, "but to be a servant, and ride behind a cab."

"Stunning, sir, I'm your man—only try me."

"I must first make some inquiries about you. Where do you live?"

"In the streets, sir."

"Surely you have some home. Where do you sleep?"

"At Daddy Spindle's when I've tin, in the streets when I aint, sir."

The gentleman started, and appeared to make a mental note of this.

Evidently, the name of Daddy Spindle had an electrifying effect upon him.

But not desiring that the boy or his own friends either should understand this, he said carelessly—

"Where's your father and mother?"

"Never knew 'em."

"Well, then, what's your name?"

"Bob Priall, sir, at your service; and if you'll only take me, you'll find me the right sort."

"Try him," cried Lamont, "he's quite an original."

After a short conversation between the two gentlemen, Bob was sent off with one of the numerous hangers-on to men of money, with instructions to feed him, have him cleaned, put into a suit of livery, and sent to his town house in Duke-street, St. James's.

And thus Bob Priall became tiger, &c., to Mr. Henry Dashwood, Dick the Diver's enemy; for such was the name of his new master.

"S'help me never," said Bob to himself, as he was handed over to the groom and footman, to receive a few necessary lessons. "I'm in for a good thing, anyhow; if it only lasts one day, these togs will grub me for a time."

Henry Dashwood, always receiving the servile attentions of numerous servants, looked upon the poorer classes as so many people born to administer to his pleasures.

When he heard the name of Daddy Spindle, it reminded him of something of which he had thought on the occasion of Dick the Diver's visit to Ashton Lodge; and that very evening, when he returned from his sporting club, where he had invested a large amount of the coin he had taken from Dick, he sent for Bob to his room.

Bob Priall gazed round him in amazement at the well-appointed apartment, where every luxury was to be seen; and at such a comical figure with his awkwardness and his new clothes, that his master laughed saying—

"You don't seem quite at home yet, Bob; but, never mind, you'll soon get used to the place; and if you are a good lad, and do as I tell you, we shall get on very well together, I'm sure."

"I hope so, sir," said Bob, very meekly, and in a very different tone to that he had used in Newgate-street that morning.

"Tell me, Bob—do you know a boy called Dick the Diver?" he asked.

Bob stared.

"Yes, sir—do you?"

Mr. Dashwood laughed heartily at the boy's reply.

"Well, I do, Bob; but that's not the question just now. Can you take me to Daddy Spindle's, where you used to sleep?"

"Yes, sir," said Bob, nervously; "only I wouldn't like to be seen taking you there, they'd say you was a—"

"Detective—a spy, or something, I suppose," said his master. "I've no doubt of that. You needn't alarm yourself, however; show me the house, and I'll find the way into it without compromising you."

Bob didn't quite understand all this; but he fancied that it meant that he wouldn't get into any row, so he said—

"When do you wish to go, sir?"

"Now. So put on your hat, and we'll start. How far is it?"

"A long way off—in Rotherhithe, sir."

"Then we shall be late."

Bob smiled—a genuine, amused smile.

"It aint never late there, sir," he said; "one time's as good as another there. So I'll get my hat, sir, and we'll start."

Ere long they were in a Hansom cab, rattling away from the grand purlieus of the parks to the miserable dens of infamy and misery which had been the centre of what Bob had once called home.

They spoke very little on the road.

Henry Dashwood had endeavoured at first to draw from his strange young companion an account of the place he was about to visit.

But without effect.

Bob gave some little information on the subject; but either from the confused state of his brain after his rise in the world, or from his nervous fear of being discovered splitting on his old companions, he made such a muddle of it that his master ceased asking questions, and Bob was left to cogitate alone.

At length the precincts of Rotherhithe were reached, and stopping the cabman at the end of a street next that in which Daddy Spindle's kitchen was situated, they alighted.

Bob Priall looked round him, and then shrunk into the gloom of the thoroughfare.

All his street boy instincts were alive again. He was no longer the prim tiger, but the boy of the streets, driven from pillar to post, from post to pillar, afraid of the police, under the dominion of his pals.

"Follow me, sir," he said; "but don't seem to be with me, 'cos they'd think I was up to somethin'."

"But they won't know you in that dress," said Henry Dashwood.

"Maybe not," said Bob; "but they're precious artful, they are."

He went on quickly, keeping as much as he could in the shadow, until they reached a narrow passage which led from one street to the other.

Peeping down this dark avenue, which was only lighted at the end by a dull lamp, Bob beckoned to his companion, saying—

"It's all right, sir—there aint nothing to be afraid of. Follow me, and be sure that I won't lead you wrong."

Bob, of course, knew his way well, and was at the other end before his master had stumbled half the distance along the rugged pathway.

At length, however, they stood together under the murky lamp which just served to make the darkness visible.

It was here that, as I said at the end of my last chapter, Dick the Diver saw them standing together, and resolved to be on the watch.

"There's the place," said Bob Priall, pointing to the spot where the light shot up from Daddy Spindle's kitchen. "You will find the old woman in her sentry box at the bottom of the stairs. In course I don't know what you want there; but I'd see old Daddy alone if I was you, 'cos they're a rum lot down in the cellar."

But his instructions were entirely lost on his master, who, impatient to consummate some purpose best known to himself, and apparently of great importance, hurried across the road and down the steps as if the place was familiar to him.

Arrived at the box where sat the old woman whom Bob had mentioned, but who had been fully described by Dick the Diver at Ashton Lodge, he said—

"I wish to see Daddy Spindle."

Now it so happened that this was simply a familiar cognomen, by which the grotesque proprietor of the kitchen was known to the tramps and others who frequented the place, the real name of the couple being Lamb.

Naturally, therefore, Mrs. Lamb took him for a swell-mobsman or a new candidate for a berth.

"Well, sir, what can I do for you?" she said; "there's the box, we charge tuppence only, and—"

Mr. Dashwood held up his hands deprecatingly.

"My good woman," he began, "you mistake me entirely. I want simply to see Spindle on a matter of business, which will be good for him and for me."

He was about to go further than this.

Mother Spindle's face grew crimson over the whole of its fatty circumference, and she brought her huge fist down with a sounding whack on the table before her.

"Do you take me for a fool?" she cried. "Do you think I don't know that nobody but tramps and cracksmen call him Daddy Spindle? Be off, if the common room is not good enough for you."

Her visitor saw at once that argument was no use with such a woman as she was.

So producing a golden emblem of peace, in the shape of a sovereign, he placed it before her.

"Do you understand now that I want to see Spindle in private?"

It was surprising to see how the woman's face changed.

The flushings of rage were transformed by her smiles into blushes of pleasure, and she said, gushingly—

"Oh! I beg your pardon, sir, I see you are a real gentleman. Sorry I have offended; but you see, sir, our name is Lamb, and it's only the tramps and so on that calls us Spindle. I'll go and fetch my husband at once, but don't say a word about the sovereign; for you see he is very stingy, and when I wants a little drop—"

There is no knowing how long she would have proceeded in this strain had not he interrupted her.

"Not a word will I say, Mrs. Lamb; but my time is precious—pray fetch your husband at once."

Thus admonished, Mother Spindle trotted off, and in a few minutes the owner of the big head stood before Henry Dashwood.

The latter certainly never expected to meet any one he knew.

There was a mutual recognition, however, and Daddy Spindle darted back with a cry of terror, and was about to give utterance to some exclamation, when Henry Dashwood seized him by the wrist.

"Hush! none of your jolly here. Come with me."

"Where?" asked Daddy Spindle, whose legs were rattling against one another like the bones of a skeleton.

"Don't be afraid," said Dashwood. "I do not like to go into the kitchen among such a set of thieves and ruffians."

"Don't mention it," said Spindle, in a tremulous voice—"don't mention it. Here is a little room on the left. Come in there."

He opened a door, which Dashwood had not before noticed, and, entering first, lit a lamp.

This was a cosy place, such as no one would have expected to find in such a house —well furnished, and so on; in fact, a retreat where Daddy and his "lamb" retired to indulge in a little extra refreshment.

They closed the door and locked it.

What they said here during the hour they were together we need not now relate; but the first words were spoken by Daddy Spindle.

"So we meet again, after all these years. On me the hand of time has been laid with a terrible heaviness, while over you it has passed so lightly that you look no older than when we were last together."

"A truce to compliments," said he.

"Compliments between us!" shuddered Daddy Spindle; and then they sat down to business.

A full hour Bob Priall stood at the entrance of the little passage where his master had left him.

More than once he had fancied that some one was watching him, but though he glanced round him in every direction, he was unable to see any one but the policeman so constantly perambulating the street.

It was, in fact, Dick the Diver who was on the watch; but he kept so well in the shadow that no one would observe him.

At the end of the hour, Bob's master emerged from the kitchen, and came almost with a run across the road.

His eyes were glassy, his face pale as death; but a smile of horrid triumph was upon his features.

"You must be up early to-morrow, Bob," he said, talking to the boy, as they hurried along, as if he was a partner in all his secrets. "Captain Carter must be seen to-morrow morning, and he goes on board the *Valparaiso* at six."

Our readers will remember that we said in our first chapter that Captain Carter never forgot that foggy night, on the 7th of November, and that it was not the fog that reminded him of it.

True enough!

When Dick the Diver had fled from the police, he had of course left the body on the beach; and after their fruitless search was over, they returned and bore the murdered body to the dead-house.

The usual inquest was held, and the usual examination was made; but there was not the slightest clue, either by a mark on linen or by a mark on papers, to prove who the sufferer was.

The blow on the back of his head proved that he had been assassinated; so he was buried in a nameless grave, with only the words— "Found murdered in the Thames," graven on a simple cross.

Not till years after was it known who carved in the dead of the night the name of Henry Ashton.

Captain Carter, had he known the fact that it was the traveller of the *Valparaiso* who was murdered, would have been able to throw a strange light upon the whole affair.

But how could he?

On the body, as I have said, were found no papers, no watch with name engraved— nothing, save the words "H. A.;" and as those who most could tell the secret had an interest in concealing all they knew, no one, beyond the circle of people at the inquest, knew more than was told in a brief paragraph in *Lloyd's Newspaper*.

For what is more common than the finding of a mutilated body in the Thames?

Who could tell, in fact, that the blow was that of a murderer, or the concussion of his head against a barge?

True, a boy had been seen by the police rifling a dead body.

But that was nothing.

To the poor and starving a dead body presents no terrors, when there is treasure to be found by handling it.

And so the affair died out in the public mind.

Not so in the mind of Captain Carter.

Night after night since that 7th of November when he came on shore, strange visions floated through his brain.

Not a real representation of the murder, truly; but a kind of hazy realization of horrors.

He awoke at first after having watched, in the deadly lock of sleep's embrace, a man following him through strange and weary ways—a man, the outline of whose form he could see well, but whose face was always averted.

Something in this man's figure appeared familiar; and yet, when he awoke, he could not recall when and where he had seen him.

He laughed over the matter at first—said to his wife, and all to whom he narrated his dream, that it must be the effect of badly cooked suppers, and so on.

But then Captain Carter didn't always eat suppers, and abstinence brought him no relief.

The man followed him everywhere in his dreams; and so terribly did the matter at last begin to prey upon his mind, that life on shore began to be insupportable, and he looked forward to the morning which should see him once more on the deck of the *Valparaiso*, getting up steam for New York.

He was sitting at supper—his last meal before starting on board by six on the morrow—when the tidings were brought to him that the good ship *Valparaiso* was on fire.

He started up, with his face all aflame.

"On fire! egad! I must be there, then," he cried, as he dashed on his jacket. "Why, hang the careless lubbers! No wonder that men dream. On fire, and we were to start by six in the morning!"

In that instant the whole scene flashed across the brain of the captain, who loved his ship as he loved his wife.

He could in fancy see the flames starting up to the sky, lapping and licking along the rigging, and sending a blood-red glow across the waters.

He could see the bustle—the men hurrying to and fro—the crowd cheering on their efforts—the whole water-side aglow with excitement; and dashing down the stairs, with scarce a word of farewell, he found at the door waiting for him a man he did not know.

"Good evening, skipper," said the fellow, in a husky voice—"bad news; ship's a-fire in two places!"

"Well, then—lead on then," cried Carter; "what's the use of standing gaping there? It's a mile to the shore. How did you come here?"

"Cab, skipper—there you be," he said, and he pointed to a Hansom which was drawn up some little distance off beneath a lamp-post.

The captain asked no further questions; but hurrying on, entered the vehicle, quickly followed by the man, who exchanged a sign with the cabman as he jumped up.

Then, in a few minutes they were whirling along the road in a direction very different from that which would have taken them to the river.

But the captain was far too excited to notice this.

He rattled on, asked a dozen questions in a minute, and, almost answering them himself, went on again, never observing that the man made the most clumsy attempts at description, and always evaded giving any specific idea of the disaster.

At length, after they had proceeded at a rapid rate along a dark road, the cab made a sudden swerve to the right, and after dashing through utter darkness came to a dead stop.

The captain, brought suddenly to his senses by this operation, glanced out.

"Why, thunder and stones!" he cried—"this is not the river-side!"

"Yes, the nearest point through yonder alley—right slick down to the water," cried the man.

"The sky's very dark," said the captain; "there can't be much of a fire."

"They've put it out, maybe," replied the man; "but let's hurry up."

The skipper, not without some misgivings, leaped from the cab, and followed his strange guide through the narrow passage, into which the man plunged with an air of pretended eagerness and haste.

There was not a particle of light anywhere in this thoroughfare; and, as the skipper stumbled along over its rugged stones, a strange misgiving came over his mind.

The dream of the last few nights once more recurred to him.

What if this stranger were the unknown being of his visions, whose face he had never seen, but whose distinct form had filled him with horror!

The idea had scarcely formed itself in his mind, when he felt something flung over his head; a stifling sensation overcame him, and he sank back into the arms of some one who had crept up behind him.

No other violence was offered to him—he was simply lifted off his feet, carried rapidly along; and then, by the warmth, he knew he was in a room, where he heard the murmur of voices.

Then he heard the scuffling of feet; and silence reigned for a time.

It was in vain that he endeavoured to escape from the foldings of the sack or whatever it was that enveloped him.

He was secured tightly round the neck and feet; and after endeavouring to shout, he relapsed into a state of quiet suspense.

Presently, he heard the door open, and two persons enter.

In another moment the sack was removed from him, and he was raised and placed in a chair.

One bewildered glance round him told him he was in a strange den.

It was, in fact, a room which had been denuded of all pretence of furniture, except a table and two chairs. The paper had been stripped off the walls, black beams crossed the ceiling, and where the fireplace had been, the iron had been torn away and sold, and a few cinders burned upon the rough brickwork.

The men before him were utter strangers apparently; for not the slightest recognition passed between him and them.

One of them, in fact, was the man who had fetched the captain in the cab.

The other was a much younger person; but his slouched hat, and the collar of his coat, which was up, prevented much of his face from being seen.

The captain of the *Valparaiso* started to his feet.

"Why am I here?" he cried. "Why was I told that lie about my ship being on fire?"

"Because we wished you to come quietly," said the man with the slouched hat. "Be seated. We wish to ask you a few questions. All attempts at resistance or escape are useless, for these parts are not much frequented by the police; and if they *did* come they would not hear your cries. So be reasonable, do all we ask, and no harm shall befall you."

## CHAPTER IX.

### A DREADFUL DEED.

ULLY persuaded, from the determined manner of the men by whom he had been entrapped, that it would be utterly useless at present to attempt resistance, Captain Carter sat down, saying—

"Speak your wishes, and be quick about it, for this is not a place at all after my heart."

"In the first place, then," said the man in the slouched hat, "you are the captain of the *Valparaiso*, which anchored in the Pool on the 7th of November?"

"I am—though I cannot—"

"Never mind, do not interrupt. You had on board several passengers, among them one who had resided some time in Chili, by name Henry Ashton."

"Yes, I believe so. I remember the name of Ashton."

"Are you aware that he was murdered on the night of the 7th, and that his body was afterwards found being plundered on the shore?"

"Murdered!" cried the captain, aghast; "now, then, I can understand my dream. Never since that night have I rested tranquilly in my bed. But why has there been no inquiry, no—"

"Because, my friend," said the other, "matters have been arranged too well. That body was found by a boy, and robbed of all money and papers; so that all the inquiries made by the police were useless. He is buried and forgotten by some; but there are others who still think of him and dream of punishing his murderer."

"And why am I here, what good can I do in the matter, except to expose all I know and aid in the search publicly?"

"That is exactly what you must not do," said the stranger; "the matter has been investigated, an inquest held, and we do not wish to have a re-opening of the verdict. Some foolish person has thought proper to advertise for you, and request you to give information. This, now, would be absurd; and so we have brought you here for the purpose of requesting your signature to this paper."

And with these words he spread a document on the rickety table.

It read as follows:—

"I, Captain Carter, being about to sail for America, in the ship *Valparaiso*, and not desiring to be detained in England, do hereby solemnly declare that no person of the name of Henry Ashton came by my vessel from New York, nor any person purporting to be a friend or relation of Henry Ashton. I make this declaration willingly, in the presence of Mr. Henry Dashwood and my mate, Robert Olsford, now discharged."

The captain glanced in amazement at the man who had fetched him in the cab, and who now, throwing off his hat and other disguises he had used, appeared before him in *propria persona*.

"Why, Olsford! what do you do here?" he said.

The man made a kind of burlesque sign of respect.

"Why, you see, cap'en," he said, "I've left the *Valparaiso* for good—taken French leave, as ye may call it; and I take my sailing orders now from this new skipper."

"I see you are in some ruffianly conspiracy," cried Captain Carter, passionately; "if it were not so, you would have come to me in a straight and above-board way and said your say. As it is, I don't like the bearings at all, and so I refuse—point blank, refuse."

Henry Dashwood—for such the other one had declared himself to be—leaned over the table, and looked Captain Carter full in the face.

"If you want to sail to-morrow morning in the *Valparaiso*," he said, "I'd advise you to sign."

There was not so much in the words, but the manner was enough to prove what cruel, steadfast resolution was in the man's mind.

Captain Carter saw it, and a strange emotion stirred his heart.

There was no doubting what this man meant, for death—murder was in his eyes; and yet the brave old salt would not yield.

"Villains!" he cried, starting up; "I can see readily what you mean, but I refuse—in the very teeth of danger, I refuse. Let me go, or I will call for aid."

"Sign, dotard," cried Dashwood, savagely. "I tell you, all hope of aid is vain. You are here caged—imprisoned, and not a living soul can hear your voice, no matter how high you may pitch it. Sign, and have done with preaching."

"Never," cried the brave old sailor — "never! And thus I will force my way among such villains!"

He drew, as he spoke, a revolver from his pocket, and aimed it at Dashwood's head, but in vain.

In an instant the floor gave way beneath his feet, and a loud splash mingled with the heavy groaning cry of dread surprise.

A yawning gulf was at the feet of the two murderers.

For an instant all was still.

Then Henry Dashwood, turning away with a shiver from the opening, from which issued a cold steam as from a charnel-house, said—

"Quick, Bob, pull up the chain, and close the trap. I'm not such a cool hand as you are."

Olsford knelt down and began pulling at the old rusty chain, by which it had been usual to draw the trap into its place.

"Curse the thing," he cried, "it won't act. Oh, horror!—help!—what's this?"

And with a gasping cry of dread he plunged to his feet.

Henry Dashwood, glancing round at that moment, saw a sight which he never afterwards forgot.

Grasping with one hand the chain, and with the other the edge of the trap door, was the old skipper, his hair matted with the ooze and slime into which he had fallen, and blood pouring down his ghastly features.

Such a terrible blow had he received by his fall into the river-side cellar, that he could not speak; but stood there, or rather was suspended there, white and horrible, with his eyes glaring with speechless hope, anxiety, fear, and wistful entreaty.

Only for an instant the two men stood looking at the ghastly object; then, at a sign from Dashwood, who seemed bereft like their victim of all speech, he raised the end of the heavy chain and dashed it in the face of the skipper.

This was the end.

There was only a convulsive clutching of the hands, and then the unfortunate man fell down into darkness and silence.

"Ugh!" shuddered Henry Dashwood as the trap-door rattled into its place—"ugh! this is a horrible job! Give me some brandy."

The brandy and two cracked glasses were soon placed upon the table, and the two men drank a goodly draught.

"And so, Henry," said the murderer of the traveller, familiarly, after he had swallowed his spirit, and leaned back in his chair and crossed his legs, without any reference to the wretched creature down below in the darkness of that living sepulchre—"so, Henry, after all these years we meet again."

"Yes," replied Harry Dashwood—"yes, we meet again. This time I am the best in pocket. Listen, and I will tell you how to be as well off as I am. Hark! what's that?"

They both listened; but it was only the howling wind which had roused them, and made them tremble in coward fear. And so, after another draught of raw spirits, they drew their chairs closer together, and in whispers began their guilty conference.

---

## CHAPTER X.

IN WHICH BOB PRIALL HAS A LARK, AND SUFFERS SOMETHING BY WAY OF RETRIBUTION.

SOME few days after the terrible event narrated in my last chapter, Harry Dashwood again visited Rotherhithe.

All again had gone well with this villain.

The disappearance of Captain Carter had, of course, created a great wonderment among the public, and some sorrow among his friends; but the wretches had so well planned their scheme that not even a suspicion of foul play, or at any rate of its authors, could be traced in the minds of any.

The *Valparaiso*—delayed, of course, a day by the extraordinary non-appearance of its captain—sailed on the following morning; for business waits for none, and out of the great waste of toiling humanity one atom taken counts for little.

Who would miss a grain of sand from the hour-glass of time?

So, though the papers commented largely upon the mysterious murder, and the advertisement which seemed to connect the night-christened victim with the ship whose captain had disappeared, the matter died out, and Robert Olsford and Henry Dashwood went on their way as before.

So now, on this night, the latter, fearless of all recognition and detection, jumped into his "swell" cab at Park-lane, and drove off once more towards Rotherhithe, with that imp of mischief, Bob Priall, hanging on behind.

Knowing his master was too occupied by his own thoughts to watch his movements, Bob determined to have a lark on his own account.

He procured a stout rope, painted black, with a ring at each end.

One of these rings he slipped on to a strong hook he had screwed to the side of the little board on which he stood; the other ring he held in his hand ready to throw on to anything that came within his reach; and then, if he could not disengage it in time, he could stoop down and slip the ring off his own hook.

It was not long before an opportunity occurred.

At the bridge a slight stoppage took place with omnibuses and cabs, one of which was slowly travelling on with a number of boxes on the top, besides a large fir tree in a flower-pot, and a perambulator, the handle of which stood temptingly forward.

On to this, with a well-directed throw, Bob slipped a ring, and at the same time his master—impatient at the delay—gave his horse a slight touch with the whip.

The sudden start brought down the perambulator, flower-pot and boxes, and in a moment all was confusion.

"Now then, stupid, where are you a-coming to?" shouted the cabby to an omnibus driver, who was standing still.

"Oh, my tree!" cried a woman from the cab.

In the midst of all, Dashwood's horse reared up, whilst Bob was disengaging the ring from the perambulator, which was hanging down by the side, and had just succeeded, when, in the act of stooping, the sudden jerk pitched him into a cart of hot meat and eel pies.

Smash went the dishes; and before the driver well knew what was the matter, Bob had climbed out and was standing at the head of his master's horse, patting him.

"Woa, Gipsy, woa!" he cried, and the noble creature gently pawed the ground, for Bob knew how to manage horses.

"What's all this uproar? Come, move on," cried a policeman, bustling up.

"Take his number," said the driver of the meat pie cart, "he's smashed all my pies."

"Who did it?" cried the policeman.

"Miles's boy! I seed him," shouted a street sweeper.

"Where is he?" said another policeman, rushing to the spot and looking wildly about.

"Sold again!" bawled out the boy, darting between the vehicles.

Bob, in the meantime, ran round the cab, jumped up, and coiling himself in by the dashboard, said—

"Drive sharp, sir, it's all right."

"What have you been up to, you imp of mischief?" said Dashwood, leaning over to Bob, and laughing, in spite of his serious thoughts, at the scene of confusion around.

"Nipping a kid's chaise off the top of a cab, getting up a fight, and tumbling into a cart of meat pies, that's all, sir," said Bob.

"A neat all, too. But be careful. We can't afford time to be stopped in the streets by your pranks. Hold on, I mean to drive fast."

And suiting the action to the word, he lashed his horse, and away they flew at a spanking pace.

As soon as they had reached the neighbourhood of Daddy Spindle's kitchen, Bob was surprised at finding his master swing round a corner and drive into a livery stable-yard.

Here he alighted, called loudly for the ostler, and delivered up trap and horse to his care, much, as may be imagined, to Bob's surprise.

Then he beckoned the lad to follow him, and when he reached the street he placed in his hand five shillings.

"Bob," he said, "I have most important business in this neighbourhood, which may detain me some hours, perhaps all night; so go and get yourself a bed, and mind behave yourself, and don't disgrace me."

"No, sir," said Bob, delighted with the possession of so much coin at once; "but what time do you want me in the morning, sir?"

"At six, at the livery stables. I have arranged with the man to let you in. Now, go on; and to-morrow when we reach home you shall have another five shillings for holding your tongue."

Delighted at this prospect, Bob touched his cockaded hat and walked away.

Arrived at a dark corner, where he was beyond the possibility of his master's seeing him, he stopped to think.

"Now, what shall I do?" he said to himself, eyeing his money lovingly. "I don't want all this for a bed. I'll pay a tanner, and I'll—"

He stopped suddenly.

A happy thought had struck him.

His heart, in fact, had yearned towards Daddy Spindle's kitchen; for there he could display his livery, and celebrate his good luck, and spend his money in treating old pals.

"Nothing like it," thought he. "It'll be all right, and master'll never know it."

And he turned slowly in the direction of the old ruined house.

Suddenly, as he went, he came face to face with a thin boy about his own age, who, stooping down, with his hands on his knees, his head stuck forward, and his body half-bent, cried—

"S'help my fish and taters, if that aint my be-looming friend, Bob Priall."

It was the voice of the Joyful Haddock, and Bob knew it well.

Why this boy should have been named after the title of an exhilarated fish it would be difficult to say, except that he was flabby in his joints, and limp in his movements, and glassy in his eyes, and yelled "Fish, oh! alive, oh!" with hideous solemnity, hour after hour every day.

Otherwise he was the reverse of his name. Joyfulness must have been absent on a tour when he entered the arena of life; so, having failed to make a friend of him early in existence, he made acquaintance with a kind of ghastly, hollow merriment, and stuck to him ever after.

"Yes, my Joyful Haddock," replied Bob, "it is me, and I'm going to the kitchen."

"What, in them togs?"

"Why not? Yes—I'm going in them. I can't well go without."

The Joyful Haddock, whose other name was Jack Lighter, hereupon uttered a howl, which was supposed by him to be a laugh, but which was enough to wake any one from their slumbers who was afraid of wild beasts.

"S'help me!" he shouted, "oh, my! oh, dear! Why, what will they think? They'll say you're some nateral curiosity."

"They may," said Bob, proudly; "but I'm a-earning a honest living, and they aint got no occasion to say much to that. Leastwise, as I aint a-going there without treating 'em."

"Oh, if that's the case," said the Joyful Haddock, "your majesty will be most welcome, I know. I will go on, and tell them you are coming."

And, with a mock bow, he dashed off in the direction of Daddy Spindle's.

For an instant Bob hesitated.

Was it safe, in fact, to trust himself there, after the mock heroics of the Joyful Haddock?

"The man who hesitates is lost," says the proverb; and so apparently thought Bob. At any rate, his pride and self-glory overcame his fear of ridicule, and within a few minutes he had paid his twopence into Mother Spindle's box, and was in the centre of the room.

He was received with acclamations of applause, and the young man with the ash-coloured hair, of whom I have before spoken, headed a kind of deputation of congratulatory friends.

"Welcome, my cockatoo," he cried, as he admiringly touched the cockade upon his hat—"welcome, my royal beast—the tiger of the desert. What are you going to stand?"

"Anything up to a crown," said Bob, proudly; and breaking through the crowd of impertinent gazers, he marched to the fireplace, and took a seat near the huge frying-pan.

He was soon the centre of an amused and admiring group.

Beer and gin having been sent for, they plied him with drink and questions; and as soon as his tongue was loosened by the mixture of liquids, he began to recount deeds of prowess and wonderful adventures in which his master and himself figured on equal terms.

Just as he was narrating an account of how he and Mr. Dashwood had been caught tipsy along with the Prince of Wales in St. James's, the ashen-haired youth opened the ball.

Carefully he began to remove the cockade from Bob's hat, and substitute in its place a bunch of white and coloured paper supplied to him by a girl selling children's toys.

Then, at a sign from him, one of the others wiped his fingers on the frying-pan, and saying, "Why, Bob, how are you?" he smeared his forehead with long streaks.

And so they kept it up: one blackening him, another attaching a piece of paper to his coat tail, another placarding his back, until at length he looked more like the sign of a rag shop with a red nose than a genuine tiger.

As for himself, Bob was quite unconscious.

"This is very jolly, my pals," he stuttered. "I shall often meet you under sim-shimilar cir-circumstances."

"Where do you live?" asked the fellow with the ashen hair.

Bob subsided into his chair, and scratched his head.

But this operation did him apparently no good, for after a few minutes he stammered—

"D-hon't know—d-hon't know."

"I know where he came from," cried the Joyful Haddock. "Let's carry him there, and prop him up against the door. They'll think that he's a guy that lost his way on the fifth of November, and has been wandering ever since. Hoist him on a chair and carry him out."

Regardless of the fact that the chair was Daddy Spindle's property, they were about to hoist Bob Priall up and carry him from the kitchen in true Guy Fawkes' fashion, when an unearthly cry—a shriek as of some person in agony and mortal terror—caused them all to stand still, with Bob drunk and decorated in their midst.

Then, as they listened for a repetition of the sound, Daddy Spindle came rushing through the secret door near the fireplace.

"Oh! help—help!" he cried, shaking his hands aloft in horror. "There's something horrible in the cellar! Help—help!"

---

## CHAPTER XI.

### THE SECRET SEVEN—A NEW MYSTERY.

"OOD morning, Tim. I hope the champagne of last night has not taken away your appetite for breakfast?" said Mr. Gregory Greed to his partner, Mr. Timothy Tact, as he entered the handsomely furnished parlour of Golden Lodge, St. John's-wood.

"No fear of that, Greg, my boy. I'm as hungry as a parson after a fat living," he replied.

The table was spread with broiled ham, eggs, and cold chicken, to which they both did ample justice.

Messrs. Greed and Tact were general and commission agents—a calling as full of cross lines and as difficult of solution as Bradshaw's Railway Guide.

They had offices in Mincing-lane, and a large brass plate boldly announced this fact to the mixed society of a shrewd and credulous public.

They were also the ruling stars of a clique called the Secret Seven, composed of men of the up-to-all-the-dodges-of-the-day class.

Having despatched their breakfast, Mr. Greed commenced reading the *Times*.

"Any drawing advertisements to-day?" said Tact, alluding to the wants that daily appear.

"Here's a handsome douceur to be given by the advertiser to any gentleman procuring him a Government appointment. Address, A. L., Peele's Coffee-house. Make a note of it."

Tact entered this in a book under the head "To be inquired into," for they worked upon a regular system, and all was fish that came to their net.

Several other items were entered, and they went to their offices in the city.

An elderly man and a boy were the only persons employed by them.

The man was a little, wizen-faced fellow, who had been transported, and returned on ticket-of-leave.

With all the pomp of purse-proud city merchants, Greed and Tact entered their office.

"Anything fresh to-day, Nip?" said Tact, addressing the old man, whose name was Thomas Nip.

"There's been a gentleman here inquiring for you several times, sir," said Nip; "here's his card."

Gregory Greed eyed the card with a knowing look; and as he did so, a smile of peculiar import flitted over his saturnine features.

"Ah!" he said, "I think I know why he has called. A piece of business just in our line, Timothy," he added, turning to his partner. "Ah! there's his knock again. Show him into our private room, and let no one disturb us."

The partners then hurried into their room, and by the time they had seated themselves by the cosy fire, Mr. Henry Dashwood was announced.

"Good morning," cried Greed, rising, and extending his skinny hand. "We expected you quite. Sit down, pray."

"Yes, sit down, pray," echoed Tact, poking the fire.

His partner had done the welcoming business, so he was not obliged to interfere in any way.

"Let me see, it is *apropos* of this fellow Daly you wish to speak, I think," said Greed; "he that lives at Myrtle College, Sydenham. He's in a furnished house there, Tact, waiting for some one who has promised his patronage. Poor as a rat, though—poor as a rat."

"Yes," said Henry Dashwood, "he *is* poor, and—of course we understand each other, or I should not speak so plainly—I want to use his poverty for a purpose. He's proud—very; and I wish his pride to be humbled in the dust."

Gregory Greed rubbed his hands together approvingly at this.

"Quite so, quite so," he said; "your ideas do your head honour, Mr. Dashwood. But tell me plainly what you wish us to do?"

"He owes you money?"

"Yes, a little."

"Well, that is one thing in favour of my proposal," said Dashwood. "But, to explain things better, I will tell you this: at present Daly is in a position of great difficulty; he has lost all by speculation; he is unfit for business; and even if he were not, he would not be able to set up in anything for want of coin. His only hope is in the promises he has received from the Honourable Moy Carruthers to place him in a Government office. Meanwhile, all his money is going; in order to keep up appearances he is living in an expensive furnished house. And if he doesn't soon obtain some aid, nothing but ruin stares him in the face. It is not for himself that he cares, but for his wife and his daughter."

"Yes, yes, I see," said Greed, with an obnoxious smile. "I begin to behold daylight. He has a beautiful daughter, and you wish to get him into a confounded mess, so that you can come forward at the right moment to save him, and claim the hand of the lovely—"

"A truce to such folly," cried Henry Dashwood, testily. "You know I am already married, and that what you say is all nonsense. I have my own ideas in the matter, of course; but I keep them to myself."

"Quite right," murmured Timothy Tact, without turning his head.

"In expectations he is rich," pursued Dashwood—"the disputed Ashton property will come to him, of course; there is no doubt that he will gain the day. I feel it lost already. But through my plan I can see a ready method of saving even that. So now I leave it in your hands. Do your best. Get this Daly in such a fix that he is helpless within a week, and I will give you fifty pounds for the job. Here is ten on account."

Greed pocketed the money with glee, and, rubbing his hands, said—

"It shall be done, Mr. Dashwood—it shall be done. It is a ticklish job, you know; but it is a pleasure to work for a gentleman like you, who always pays."

"Besides, you may call me one of the Secret Seven," said Dashwood, with a smile. "Since Cooper Evans died, I've given you more information than any one in the city. Good morning, Mr. Greed—good morning, Mr. Tact. I shall expect to hear from you ere a week is over your head."

He then took his departure, leaving the two partners in mirthful glee. Little, indeed, did Dashwood know how easy was the task he had assigned to them to perform.

He had, indeed, scarcely left the room when Thomas Nip entered, saying—

"Sharp's just called to say that Brown hasn't paid this week, and that you must go in at once."

Tact and Green exchanged glances, as well they might, for Brown was the landlord of Daly's furnished house.

"By all means," cried Greed. "A man that doesn't keep his payments good on a bill of sale must abide the consequences. Here, boy, run to Mr. Snatch, and tell him to come here directly."

Snatch, broker and appraiser, another of the Secret Seven, soon made his appearance.

"Take two vans and men immediately to Myrtle Cottage, Sydenham, and bring away Mr. Brown's goods."

"All right—that's business, there's nothing like being down upon them at once. No shilly-shally, with a few days' grace, and all that soft-hearted humbug. A clean sweep and a quick return, that's the style for me."

Snatch set about his task with pleasure, for nothing he delighted in so much as selling people up.

In his own bills of sale he had a clause that unless the landlord's rent was paid within three days after date, he had the power of taking their furniture.

Many a family knows this to their cost; and upon the ruin and misery of others, Snatch is building up a fortune for himself, without a thought or care for their sufferings, so long as he makes money.

And there are thousands like him, who go on cheating and thriving in a worldly sense, without reflecting that one day they must give up all; for Death presents a bill that admits of no renewal.

Snatch and his men, and two vans, stopped at Myrtle Cottage.

"Mr. Brown within?" said Snatch, rudely, entering the house.

"Mr. Brown does not live here, sir," replied a servant maid.

"That be hanged for a tale! Come, it's no use attempting any humbug with me. I come on the part of the Assistance to All Men Loan Society."

"I know nothing about it, sir. I'll call Mrs. Daly, if you'll wait a minute."

Saying which she ran down to call her mistress.

"What is your business, sir?" said Mrs. Daly, hastily appearing.

"I've come for Mr. Brown, mum."

"He is not here, sir."

"Well, then, I must follow out my instructions. Here is my authority, mum," said Mr. Snatch, showing the bill of sale.

"I don't understand it, sir."

"Can't help that, mum. The law must take its course. Business is business, mum. Mr. Brown hasn't paid his browns, and the Assistance to All Men Loan Society don't brown to that. Now, Potts, call in the other men, and let's to work."

The man Potts, alluded to, beckoned to half a dozen men outside, who immediately entered.

"Good Heaven!—what do you mean?" exclaimed Mrs. Daly, in alarm.

"Mean?—why to clear out, to be sure. Come, Potts, two in a room, and look sharp."

"Stop, my good sir. Mr. Daly took this house furnished, for three months, of Mr. Brown, and paid twenty pounds in advance. Here is the receipt."

"That's your business, mum; and it appears Mr. Brown has done you brown! But that's not my business."

"Surely you'll wait till my husband returns?"

"Can't, really. Unless you pay me one hundred pounds, I must remove everything in the house."

"No, no; you never will act so cruelly."

"Won't I, though. We'll soon see about that. Cruel, indeed! I should like to know what kindness a man expects who doesn't pay his way?"

"Well, but we don't owe the money."

"But you're in the house of the man that does, which is sufficient for me."

Mr. Snatch now commenced in earnest. Bedsteads were taken down, beds tied up and thrown downstairs, chairs and tables carried out; and in an incredibly short space of time the house was stripped.

Mr. Daly had that day invited a number of friends to dinner, among them two persons upon whom his future depended.

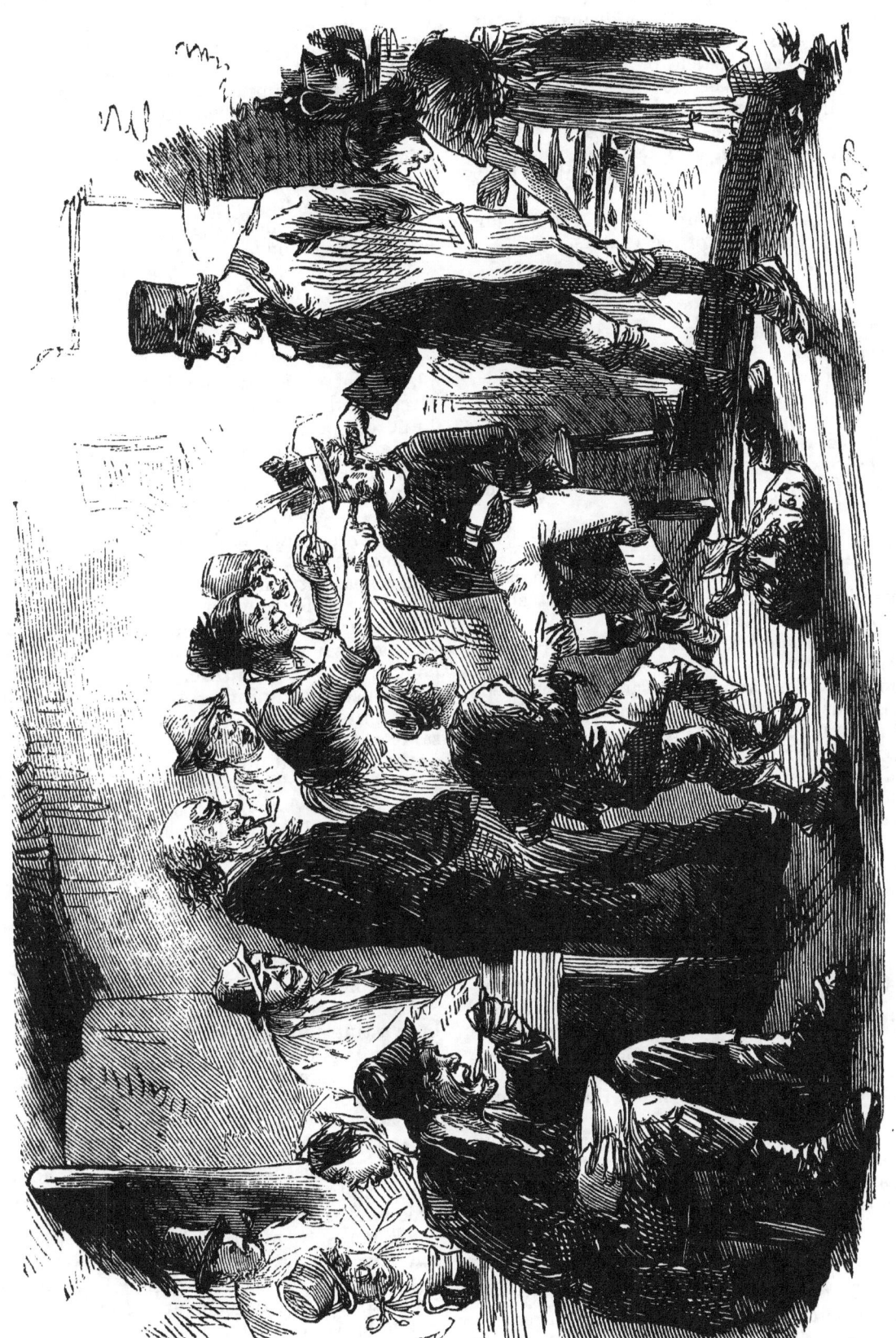

HOW BOB PRIALL WAS DECORATED BY HIS FRIENDS.

A fine turkey and sirloin of beef were roasting, pies and tarts were in the oven, when Snatch, to the utter dismay of the servant, packed up dishes, plates, knives, forks, and every article of use, leaving the meat and turkey before the fire, with the gravy dripping on the hearthstone.

Only a few boxes, with Mr. Daly's name painted upon them, were left.

Sitting upon one of these, Mrs. Daly awaited her husband's return.

Two cabs drove up, and a rat-tat announced the arrival of the visitors.

"Run and open the door, Mary, and show them into the parlour."

"Lor', mum, the room be quite empty!"

"Never mind. I must tell them what has happened."

Upon explaining the case to her friends, one exclaimed—

"Why, the thing's impossible!"

"It doesn't appear like it, when I haven't a chair to ask you to sit down upon," said Mrs. Daly. "But here comes my husband."

Mr. Daly was equally astounded; but as the thing was done, all that remained was to adjourn to the nearest hotel and entertain his visitors, though his heart, as may well be imagined, bled at the expense.

The next day he called at the office of the Assistance to All Men; and ascertaining, however harsh and unpleasant their proceedings, they had the law upon their side, he was compelled to put up with the loss.

On reaching home, which was now a suite of furnished apartments in a neighbouring house, he found Henry Dashwood awaiting him.

---

## CHAPTER XII.

### A DEADLY INFLUENCE.

SHADE of something like annoyance overspread the face of Algernon Daly as he came into the room where sat his visitor; but it quickly vanished in the hope that sprung up in his heart that this man might aid him.

"Good morning, Mr. Caleb Stringer," said he, addressing Dashwood by an evidently assumed name; "you find me in the middle of a sad affair."

"Ah!" said Dashwood, "it is, indeed, sad; but we must find means to remedy the matter."

"Impossible, impossible!" cried Daly, in a melancholy voice; "nothing can ever remedy the evil done in regard to the Honourable Moy Carruthers. He little knew that I was in a furnished house, and had invited one of his own special friends to my dinner party. When these accursed brokers' men had cleared everything out, nothing would convince him of the truth. He was cold, distant, and reserved, and left immediately dinner was over. In that quarter I am ruined."

"Money can do anything, my dear friend," said Dashwood; "so do not despair. If you can't get patronage by acting as a gentleman, you must buy it."

"You mock me, Caleb," said Daly; "you know I have none."

"That is no reason why your friend should have none," returned Dashwood. "I can, I think, arrange a little matter for you. We'll take another house—or, better still, some grand apartments in London. Then we'll place the matter in the hands of Messrs. Greed and Tact—my agents; give them a hundred pounds, and they'll guarantee to get you a permanent and gentlemanly situation in less than six months. I'll give you a cheque now for three hundred. Don't be surprised—don't thank me. I've just happened on a mine, as the Yankees would say —come, in fact, into some money; so I can easily spare it, and you can pay me when you come in for your luck."

Of course Daly was profuse in his thanks. In his own mind he would rather have bought Brown's furniture, and gone back to the house in triumph; but this would not have suited Dashwood's plans. And as he said it would be "infra dig.," and poohpoohed it, he did not press the matter.

Business having been concluded, the two men adjourned to the room where sat the ladies—namely, Mrs. Daly and her daughter Alice.

The former was a woman about forty years of age, bearing a striking resemblance to Mrs. Henry Dashwood; while the latter was a girl of some eighteen summers, lovely more in her intellectuality and her grace than in her absolute beauty.

Her form was petite; her hair was of a light brown tint, falling in careless abandon over her slight but prettily rounded shoulders; her eyes were of a bright hazel, while her complexion was of an olive hue, radiant ever and anon as with the glow of an Italian sky.

Both the ladies received Dashwood warmly, but Alice with marked attention—her cheeks being suffused with blushes and her eyes drooping in pleasure.

"Thanks to my friend Stringer, Eliza," said Algernon Daly, while a look of unalloyed happiness overspread his face, "I fancy our difficulties will soon be over. At present we are going to quit this place, and take some furnished lodgings in London; within six months I hope to have an appointment."

"But, meanwhile," said matter-of-fact Mrs. Daly, "how are we to live?"

"Fear not, my dear," returned her husband—"that, too, through Stringer—"

Dashwood raised his hand deprecatingly, while a look of conscious generosity and rectitude overspread his face.

"Say no more, friend Daly," he said; "enough of business for to-day. It is an ill wind that brings nobody good, Mrs. Daly; and perhaps this last mishap of your husband's may be the means of bringing him good fortune."

Presently Mrs. Daly was called away; and, at Dashwood's request, Mr. Daly went out to get ready for a trip to London.

The instant the door was shut, Dashwood hurried over to the spot where Alice sat in the window, and bent over her.

"Well, Alice," he said, as he took her hand, "have the spirits given you any better counsel yet?"

The young girl, whose hand lay passively in his, though her cheeks were suffused with blushes, shuddered as he spoke these words.

"They only counsel as before, Caleb," she murmured.

And yet, as she uttered the syllables—not even looking into his evil, handsome face—there was a world of sad tenderness in her tones.

He sat down beside her, after listening for footsteps.

"Alice," he said, with a low, passionate voice, "this secret—this mystery, cannot last long. I must and will know all. You cannot avoid my influence. To-morrow night, at our old trysting-place, at the usual hour, I shall expect you. I *know* you will be there!"

"I *must* be there," she said, shudderingly; "but I need not speak."

"I will trust in Fate for that," he answered, triumphantly.

But he could say no more, for footsteps were heard approaching; and he had scarcely succeeded in assuming a careless posture and demeanour, when Mr. Daly entered.

"Now, Stringer," he cried, "I'm ready, and all impatience to see Greed and Tact. Let's start at once."

The dream and its surroundings, which had so utterly altered for a moment the aspect of things, was thus rudely dispelled.

What did it mean? What new and deadly mystery was Henry Dashwood engaged in?

## CHAPTER XIII.

### THE APPARITION IN THE CELLAR—DICK THE DIVER HAS A NEW ADVENTURE ON THE RIVER.

UR readers have not forgotten that we left old Daddy Spindle rushing frantically from behind the secret opening by his fireplace, shouting—

"Help!—help! there's something horrible in the cellar."

What the old fellow was doing down in that dark region alone will be explained in due course. Whatever it was, it was evidently not of a cheering or exhilarating kind, for his face was of a ghastly hue, which was hardly to be accounted for by a sudden apparition.

For an instant the crowd which was assembled in the kitchen hesitated; but at length four of the men, including the young man with the ashen hair, volunteered to accompany him on his voyage of discovery.

Daddy Spindle led the way—his thin legs trembling, his body in a perfect convulsion of fear, his goggle eyes seeming to burst from his head.

Slowly they descended, more than one of those that brought up the rear being inclined to laugh at the whole matter—for Daddy Spindle's courage was none of the greatest; but as they reached the bottom of the staircase, if such a name can be applied to the rough steps, they all started as a low, gasping cry was heard.

"Save me, for the love of Heaven!"

"Oh! oh!" stammered Daddy Spindle, staggering back. "I can't go on, I can't indeed. It aint nothing human, that I'll swear."

"Rubbish!" cried a big, brawny ruffian who was known as Bully Wrench, "come on, old man. 'Taint no good frightening all the kitchen and then backing out. Come on— I'll protect you."

And so saying, he seized hold of the old fellow by the arm, and dragged him on in the direction of the sound.

This was in the direction of what we have already known as the Cage; and on nearing it Daddy Spindle began to tremble so violently that Bully Wrench had almost to carry him; but at length they reached it, and all rushed in, in a pushing, driving, tumultuous body.

On the wall of the cavernous cellar was stuck a sputtering candle, and all shuddered and stood still as they saw what appeared at the little grating.

A face, white and horrible, with snowy hair straggling over it—every feature besmeared with blood, flowing from a ghastly wound in the temple.

And out of the pallid lips—as the head rose and fell with the wash of the river— came the bubbling cry—

"Save me! save me!"

Daddy Spindle could stand no more; he crouched down in a corner, moaning some inarticulate words to himself; while Bully Wrench advancing, dragged the grating out of its place and peered out into the darkness —the still, solemn darkness of the river Thames.

What he saw there for an instant held him spellbound. An old man—the owner of the ghastly face—was clinging to a piece of driftwood, which floated to and fro as the water rose and fell.

Bully Wrench was not celebrated for his kindness or generosity of heart; but he felt an uncomfortable lump in his throat as the wistful eyes of the sufferer beamed up at him through the dark night.

"Here, old man—cotch hold of my hand," he said. "Never mind the spar, when yer've once cotched hold. I'm strong enough to save you. There, never fear—take a good grip."

The old man feebly seized the hand of the powerful fellow who had offered his aid, and in a few minutes he was dragged to the grating, and amid the wonderment of the kitcheners he was pulled into the cellar.

He gazed round him with a vacant stare.

"Where am I?" he said.

"In Daddy Spindle's Cage," said Bully Wrench, "where no one sha'n't harm ye any more. Come along o' me, old man. Take my arm. Have a drop o' rum and water upstairs, and then, maybe, you'll be able to tell us where you came from, and how you want to get home."

Daddy Spindle—seeing now that his visitor was really human and not a spirit—had recovered from his insane fear, and taking the spluttering light from the wall, led the way up into the kitchen, where they placed him in a cosy nook by the fire.

"It's warm here," he said, under his breath, "nice and warm here. Not like out on the river. Oh, it was terribly cold there—terrible!"

"How came you there?" cried Bully Wrench, who was brewing a drop of rum and water, paid for by himself. "You seem to have been knocked about a bit. Who did it?"

The wounded man put his hand up wearily to his head, where the gash was on his forehead.

"I can't tell," he muttered—"it seems all strange now. I can't remember anything. Don't ask me, it makes my head swim. But it was terrible—horrible down there among the rats; and I better liked the river, with all its cold and darkness."

"Here, drink this," said Bully Wrench, holding out the grog, and almost helping the old man to swallow it. "Why, you're a sailor—a captain of a vessel, or something, aint you?"

"A vessel—eh? Yes, a noble one, once; but don't talk of it, it makes my head ache. Get me to bed. I've money here; see, this is gold—good gold. If you don't believe, take it and hear it chink. All honestly earned—

all—all so hardly for the dear ones I shall never—never—never see again."

And then he bowed his head and wept.

The tramps, male and female, who crowded round him, eyed the gold wistfully: some men who had had a bad day; some women with babies at their breasts, who were more than doubtful as to the next day's meal.

But they never touched it.

Something there was in the old man's distress which went straight to their hearts, and not one was there who would not have resented any attempt at robbing him of his little store.

It was useless, evidently, to attempt to extract from him any account of who he was, where he lived, what was his name, or who were his assailants. His head, in fact, had been somewhat touched by the attack.

"It don't matter," said Bully Wrench, who, for some reason best known to himself, had taken a most lively interest in the new-comer. "He's got money, Daddy—give him a good bed, and when he's spent it all, why—dang me if he sha'n't be my pensioner!"

A murmur of applause arose from the assembled group.

But Bully Wrench evidently did not approve of this.

He turned round savagely.

"Has it got anything to do with any of you?" he said. "Mind your own business. I've got *my* reasons—mark me, and I don't choose to tell 'em; so p'raps I oughtn't to have applause at all. You'd like a dip into this pensioner, p'raps, some of you; but *I* arn't a going to touch a penny of his money, and I'm tarnation certain none of *you* shall. This way, old man, I'll show you to bed."

And so, leaning on the arm of the strong, reckless man, the poor old waif of the river tottered to his bed.

That night Dick the Diver began anew his adventures on the river, or he might have been at home in the kitchen when the arrival of the old man had created such wonderment and consternation.

He had, as we have seen, to begin life anew —penniless as before, and more friendless.

So at his usual hour he entered his little skiff, and pushed off upon the bosom of the moonlit Thames.

Often at this hour—as in the olden times —a man would pay him to ferry him across; often some wretched being, driven to madness, would plunge into the dark waters, to be rescued by Dick, and to reward him for a life which a moment before had been recklessly hazarded.

But nothing of this kind happened to him on this particular night. All seemed quiet on the river; and he was just despairing of anything but a fruitless return home, when loud and angry voices broke upon his ear.

He turned round sharply in the direction from which the sound proceeded, and saw in a house whose very walls were washed by the river a shadow on a blind as of two persons struggling.

"Here is an adventure," thought Dick; and without a moment's hesitation he pulled his boat towards the spot.

Pulling his skiff up close to the wall, he steadied himself, raised himself to a level with the window, and peered in.

A strange scene presented itself.

The room was decently—nay, comfortably —furnished, and on the table in the centre was the remains of a goodly repast.

Standing up near this was an old man of some sixty winters—a thin old man, with the appearance of having worried himself into his skinny state by constant grubbing after money.

Near him stood a young man about five and twenty, whose gestures were indicative of anger and deep annoyance; and just as Dick the Diver clung on to the window-sill and looked in, he seized the old man by the throat and raised his arm to strike.

But the blow never descended.

"Hallo!" cried Dick, "what are you up to?"

In an instant the young man turned towards the window.

"Who's there?" he shouted, savagely.

"It's only me," cried Dick; and, fearless as he always was, he swung himself up, and in an instant was by the side of the combatants.

The man released his intended victim.

"And pray, you young vagabond," he cried, "what are you doing here?"

"Well, I came here to do nothing in particular," said Dick; "but it seems to me I came just in the nick of time—just in time to hinder you doing a murder."

The man gazed at him with fury in his eyes.

"Why, you young villain, you ragged imp, how dare you?" he shouted. "Be off, or I'll dash your brains out, and fling you into the river."

He made a threatening advance upon Dick, but the boy was too wide-awake for him. He retreated a few steps, and drew from his breast a friend he had not lost with his money—his revolver.

"Back!" he said. "Don't try any games with me, or I'll fire."

The argument was as successful as it was persuasive, and the young man drew back, defeated and surly, towards the table, on a chair near which the old man had sunk breathless and exhausted.

"Dion," said the latter feebly, "I forgive you; leave me now—I would be alone for awhile."

"Turn that boy out of the window he came in by, then," said Dion.

"No, he may be useful," said the other. "Dion, go. Boy, remain."

The young man, whose fury seemed now to have spent itself, growled something apologetic, and quitted the room; when in an instant the old fellow rose, went on tiptoe to the door, locked it, and returning to the table in the same peculiar fashion, sat down, and beckoned to Dick to take a chair near him.

"Boy," he said, "you've saved my life. That's my son, Dion; but no matter for that. His temper is fearful, truly dreadful; and when he's put out, he is for the moment like a very devil. He is indeed, as sure my name is Thomas Nip."

Thomas Nip! Yes, truly a strange and wondrous coincidence. The clerk to Messrs. Greed and Tact, of Mincing-lane, City, one of the Secret Seven, of whom Henry Dashwood was one.

"Yes," continued the old man, pouring out some spirit, and offering it to Dick— "yes, Dionysius is hasty—he's a good boy, but hasty; and has more than once nearly squeezed the life out of me. But he's never done it, you see; he's always been stopped. I suppose it is not his fate to do it. He's a fine fellow, my Dion; it would be a pity for him to get into trouble. Yes, Dion's a fine fellow!"

This was said in a kind of reverie to himself, while he sipped his glass; and Dick was already cogitating about the prudence of retiring, when Thomas Nip broke out suddenly—

"Boy, have you a situation?—and if not, would you like one?"

Dick's eyes brightened.

"No, sir, I haven't got one," he said; "and I'd be glad, indeed, to earn an honest penny."

Thomas Nip made a wry face at this; but, perhaps because of his eagerness to hear more, Dick did not discern it.

"Well, so ye shall—so ye shall," he said. "You've saved my life, so I know you're a brave boy—a very brave boy; and so I know you're honest, and can keep a secret. Now, what I want you to do is very simple. There is a man who is trying to do a very wicked action, which I have a chance of preventing. He requires watching, but if I were to watch him he would guess that something was wrong, and all my plans would fall to the dust. Now, if you will undertake this office, I will pay you well."

"What am I to do, then?" asked Dick.

"Simply watch him from place to place all day, and report to me."

"I will do it, sir," said Dick, who rather appreciated the style of adventure. "How am I to begin?"

"Well," said old Thomas Nip, joining his finger ends confidentially, and speaking in a low voice, "to-morrow night, at nine o'clock, a gentleman will issue from the Albion Club in Pall Mall; he will look anxiously up and down as if waiting for some one; and then, after a minute, a carriage will drive up, which he will enter. Follow that carriage, and report to me."

"Very well, sir," said Dick. "I understand all now."

"Good boy," said Thomas Nip; "here are two or three shillings. Come here to-morrow night with a proper report, and you shall have a sovereign, and be taken regularly into my service."

"And what is the name of your street?" asked Dick. "I don't know it by this back way."

"I dare say not," said Nip; "but never mind that at present. Come here to-morrow night by the window as you came to-night. It will be safer at first. Now, go."

In a few minutes, Dick, full of his new adventure, was once more floating on the bosom of old Father Thames.

Old Nip, meanwhile, went slowly up the old rickety stairs of the house—so old-fashioned that the steps went right into the room where Dionysius Nip slept.

The brute who had so villainously attacked his father was now snoring in a semi-drunken sleep, with his head thrown back on the pillow.

The old man approached the bed with his lamp, and tenderly bent over him with glistening eyes.

"Poor boy, poor Dion!" he murmured; "he's very violent, but he's a good boy. God bless him!"

And then he passed away to his room, contented; though perhaps, had he been able to scan the future, his thoughts would have taken a far different turn.

Next night, at the appointed hour, Dick was posted opposite the Albion Hotel—in fact rather before his time; and he had an opportunity therefore of watching the busy stream of life that constantly ebbed and flowed before him—foot passengers hurrying to and fro on business; and carriages clattering by with freights of beauty for the theatre.

When the hour struck, Dick the Diver crossed over and planted himself beneath the shadow of the large portico of the Albion, where he could see every one who entered or passed out, without himself being observed.

He had not long to wait; for, indeed, he had scarcely taken up his position when a young man, handsome and of distinguished aspect, descended the steps of the club, and looked scrutinizingly round him.

He was an utter stranger to Dick; but he at once recognized him by his eager glances.

Scarcely a moment had elapsed when a carriage, drawn by two bays, dashed up to the entrance, and with a delighted look the young man hurried down to the door.

The idea had scarcely formed itself in Dick's mind—"How am I to follow this carriage through the crowded streets?" when from the carriage beamed forth a vision which sent his blood coursing madly through every vein.

It was the face of Miriam Morris, radiant with beauty, bedecked in jewels, dressed in luxurious splendour.

Forgetting all—the difference of his position, the dress he wore—he rushed forward, expecting at least a smile; but Miriam, casting one horrified glance at him, sprang to the other window, and cried—

"Quick, coachman, drive on—quick!"

And this was how Miriam and Dick Ashton met in London—she driving off in mad haste, drawn by her splendid horses; and he standing ragged and alone on the cold pavement, in the thick December mist.

Dick the Diver for a few moments stood, as it were, spell-bound by what he well considered a catastrophe.

Then he remembered his mission; and urged forward now by a double impulse—the wish to serve Thomas Nip, and the desire to discover if possible the destination of Miriam and the handsome young lounger of the club —he glanced after the departing vehicle, and seeing it blocked by some coming carriages, he rushed away in spite of the wild beating of his heart.

It naturally suggested itself again to Dick the Diver that it would be quite impossible for him to continue his pursuit of those two fiery bays along a crowded street.

But then there was only one alternative at first—to hang on behind; but against this his heart revolted. How, indeed, could he submit to such a humiliation—he outside, like a beggar boy, clinging to the rails of Miriam's carriage! Never!

Rather than this he would forego the pursuit—forego his own eagerness—forego the chance of money. But suddenly another idea presented itself.

A Hansom cab was standing by the kerb, which he at once hailed.

The cabman looked at first rather doubtfully at the woe-begone figure which thus accosted him; but Dick the Diver clinched the bargain with a vigorous argument.

"I say, cabby," he said, "I know your fare to the Opera is only a bob; follow that brougham with the pair of bays, and I'll give you three. Here they are."

The cabby, a jolly fellow, laughed.

"All right, my young detective," he cried; "jump in—quick, too, for the block's over, and they're off."

Along the busy, showy streets they pressed, and at length the Opera House was reached, and the carriage stopped to unload its freight, while Dick sprang from the cab to watch.

All was warmth, and glitter, and luxury within; but without the snow had begun to fall, and all London was being covered with a white mantle.

## CHAPTER XIV.

### DICK FOLLOWS—MISERY—THE FIRE.

ICK the Diver, after seeing Miriam and her strange companion safe within the walls of the Opera, passed across the road, and, placing himself in a doorway, watched.

It was weary waiting.

Cold and bitter as was the night, it was as nothing to the chill thoughts within him—thoughts which seemed to obliterate for ever every hope which had softened life before.

How ineffably sweet, now that they were lost for ever, seemed the evenings which he used to spend with Miriam; when Gentleman Morris used to tell his genial stories, and he used to sit by the girl who had taken possession of his heart, and hold her hand, and look up into her beaming eyes, and read a love which he deemed would be a love for ever.

Alas! the first golden breath of wealth had blown away for ever the memories of old days. She was Miriam Morris the basket-maker no longer—she was the petted heiress.

And yet—oh, Miriam!

If she had but known the precipice upon the edge of which she was standing—if she had but known how false and hollow were the promises of her new-found friends—how terrible the destiny to which she was doomed by them!

But the dream was not over. She was now, as it were, in the full delirium of success; and failure was a thing in the unknown future.

All these things rushed through the mind of Dick the Diver as he waited there in the wretched cold, watching the door of the Opera.

The snow kept pouring down.

Thicker and thicker grew the white mantle of the earth; and with the descending shower there came a driving wind which beat the wet into the passage where he stood, and soon drenched him to the skin.

But he thought not of it—in fact, he scarcely observed it. There was a chill, truly, at his heart; but it was a chill that seemed to burn.

At length the clock struck the welcome hour at which the play was over, the carriages began to get to their places, and the bustle at the doorway commenced.

Dick the Diver, in spite of the frowns of policemen, elbowed his way through the throng, and fixed himself just at the iron gates, where he could see all who passed.

Eagerly he peered into the faces of the pleasure-seekers, as they rolled off to their luxurious homes; and presently, as the carriages rolled slowly by, he saw Miriam sitting by the side of the stranger.

But in the same carriage, opposite to her, was Henry Dashwood.

The sight so startled him, that for an instant a film passed across his eyes, and he nearly fell; but he was roused from it by feeling a hand brought down heavily upon his shoulder, and by hearing a voice say—

"Halloa, Dick, have you been to the huproor? I thought so, 'cos the Hemperor of China's here, and I heard his flunkey a-saying as his carriage were a-waiting for you at the corner."

It was the Joyful Haddock that spoke; and as his unwashed palm rested in friendly familiarity on Dick's shoulder, Miriam's carriage stopped, and her eyes caught his.

At first, the pleading, wistful look in his face made her glance at him in serious fear—fear, too, lest he should spring forward, and, in spite of all, claim friendship and companionship.

But when she saw the Joyful Haddock standing by him, in all his ludicrous rags and his comic wretchedness, a smile of supreme disdain passed over her features, and she turned aside her head.

Dick the Diver was only human.

Before this nothing had filled his heart in regard to Miriam but the most devoted attachment.

Now, however, the hot blood surged from his heart to his head, the demon of anger and hate took possession of his soul for a time, and leaning his head against the iron railing, he muttered—

"Oh, I'll be revenged for this—bitterly—bitterly revenged!"

And then, dragging his companion with him, he sprang after the carriage, which had already reached the corner of Long-acre.

All ideas of pride, and so on, were banished from his mind now.

Revenge had disposed of them.

"She is cruelly unkind, ungrateful, and deceitful," he said to himself. "I'll live to make her regret it."

So, turning to the Joyful Haddock, he cried, with a forced laugh, which passed current very well with his companion—

"Here, Joyful, let's have a ride on that carriage. I want to see where they go. So, come on, and mind the spikes."

The ride was not a long one.

Back they clattered over the rough stones until they reached Park-lane, where Henry Dashwood had taken up his residence.

Here all three descended.

Miriam and the young stranger passed up the steps of the house, but Henry Dashwood remained behind awhile to give some directions.

An idea struck Dick.

This man, whom in his own heart he believed to be an impostor, had possession of his money—why not ask him for some?

Boldly he advanced when the brougham drove off.

"Mr. Dashwood," he said, "I wish to have a word with you."

Dashwood started, and glanced at him in amazement.

"Who are you," he cried, "that know my name? Come under the lamp, and let me have a look at you."

He caught Dick by the arm as he spoke, and dragged him beneath a lamp-post.

Then his face assumed a furious aspect.

"Why, you young thief and vagabond," he cried, "is it you? I will call the police. I—"

"Stop, Mr. Dashwood," said Dick; "you may call the police as much as you like. You frightened me once when I was down at Ashton Lodge, but you can't do it again. You said you would deliver me over to the police as the murderer of Mark Ashton. You have no proofs, and I defy you."

"Why, you young rascal!" cried Dashwood, "you know well that both myself and my wife know from your own statement what happened."

"Yes, and I know," said Dick the Diver— "I know that Mrs. Dashwood would never bear witness against me."

It was a mere statement, said in a quiet, simple way; but yet it seemed to bring a strange conviction to Henry Dashwood's mind.

And so he altered his tone.

"My lad," he said, with an attempt at kindness—"my lad, I forgive you for much, because you are unfortunate; but I cannot be annoyed, or bored, or followed about. You are very wretched, I have no doubt, in your present position, and I will try and get you out of it; but to-night I have no time to waste. What is it you desire to tell me? Tell me quickly, and then let me see you here to-morrow evening, after it is dark."

"Mr. Dashwood," returned Dick, "I simply want my own. I have an idea—why, I know not, but it is impressed upon my mind— that the whole of that money which you kept

from me is mine; and I now demand some of it, at any rate. I lost my twenty pounds on my road to London. I want now to receive enough to enable me to raise myself from my wretchedness, and assume that position which is really my own. *You* know, in your own heart, better than *I* do, who I am. Deal fairly with me in consequence."

Henry Dashwood listened calmly to the boy's words.

But any one who had been watching the scene would have seen at once how the passions were warring within him; and as Dick spoke the last syllables, he gripped his arm fiercely.

"Mark me, my lad," he said, "I understand your game quite well. We are alone, and your word would never in any court of law be taken against mine. Here are ten pounds; these are the last you will ever get from me. I don't believe a word about your losing your money; but I do believe that you fancy you've sprung a mine. You're wrong. Trouble me again, and I'll chance all you can do."

Dick the Diver pocketed the money, and flung away the unfriendly grasp.

"I take this money, Mr. Dashwood," he said, quietly, "to aid me in having my revenge. I know well the enemy I have to deal with. You need never fear that I will again ask for anything, until I ask for all; but remember this, I am not so much alone in the world as you think."

Henry Dashwood muttered something between his teeth, and moved away.

Dick stood and watched him until he entered the door—the door through which Miriam had passed, but which was not to be opened to *him;* and then, forgetful of all but what had just occurred, he was about to turn away, when he saw an object by the side of him which, in spite of his melancholy, made him laugh.

It was the Joyful Haddock, standing on his head!

"What are you doing?" cried Dick. "I'd forgotten you were here."

"'Xactly so," said the Joyful, "but, you see, I've heard all that bloke's palaver. I can squint through a milestone perhaps as well as any one, and I know he's a villain. You said one good thing though, Dick," he added, righting himself, and digging his friend in the ribs.

"What's that?" asked our hero.

"You said you was not so much alone in the world as *he* thought, Dick—no more you aint, old chum. The Joyful Haddock is *your* pal—*your* friend, and his enemy as long as he breathes, or else—so help me never!"

And to clinch the argument, he performed three Catherine wheels on the snowy pavement.

DICK RAISED HIMSELF TO A LEVEL WITH THE WINDOW AND PEERED IN.

In spite of his misery, Dick could not help laughing at his eccentric friend.

"Come along," he said, "come on! There's nothing to stop for now, and besides, I've got to see my employer."

"Employer!" cried the Joyful Haddock, as they shuffled on through the snow. "Why, you're getting quite a rich swell."

"Yes, I made that villain shell out properly," he answered; "and, by the way, take this sovereign, Joyful, and you can get some clothes, and so on, and perhaps drop in for some employment too."

The Joyful took the coin, spun it in the air, at the imminent risk of losing it in the snow. Then he bit it, held it under a lamp; and concluded his performance by placing it in his pocket, and giving a prolonged whistle.

"Well, so help me never!" he cried, "if this aint been a good night. If I hadn't a-happened to ha' met you, I should have had to eat a sausage and bread for supper; but now I'll have a good blow out, and I'll invite you and Bully Wrench to supper, 'cos he saved the old man from the kitchen sharks. Come on, and let's get your business over quick."

## CHAPTER XV.

IN WHICH DICK AND THE JOYFUL, INSTEAD OF HAVING SUPPER, MEET WITH ANOTHER STRANGE ADVENTURE.

THE two boys trudged along quickly; and Dick having changed a sovereign at a public-house, they engaged another wondering cabman, and were not long in reaching the precincts of Rotherhithe.

Here they dismissed the man, and hurrying along to the waterside they entered a boat and pulled towards the house of the mysterious Thomas Nip.

When they reached it, a light was burning in the window, as a signal to Dick that the old man had not retired to rest.

"How do you get in?" asked the Joyful Haddock. "Isn't it better to go round the front way?"

"No, that's against orders," replied Dick. "This is some very mysterious business—more than I can understand, I can tell you; and when I visit him, I am always to go by the window. Steady, pull up—there!"

Dick rose, took a firm hold of the window sill, and tapped on the glass.

In an instant the blind was drawn up, and the old man appeared.

"Good boy—good boy!" he cried, as he opened the casement, "come in. I've been anxiously expecting you."

Dick leaped in, and, the window being closed, he sat down by the fire which glowed in the old-fashioned grate.

"Now, then, boy," said Nip, "help yourself to a little drop of that brandy—you must be cold after your waiting about in the snow —and tell me all you have discovered."

"Not much, as it appears to me," said Dick the Diver; "but it may seem different to you."

Circumstantially, he narrated all the events of the evening—the old man rubbing his hands, and swaying to and fro, with a strange smile upon his face.

"This is all very interesting to me," said he, when Dick had narrated all—excepting, of course, his private interview with Dashwood. "So you say that the young lady and the gentleman who came from the club door went to the Opera together."

"Yes."

"And the other returned with them?"

"Yes."

"I see it all, then—an artful trap of Dashwood's; but no matter, we'll cheat him— we'll defeat him," exclaimed Nip, with glee. "That young man—Lord Eustace Andover, must be saved."

"Saved!" echoed Dick, in surprise. "Why, I know Miriam Morris. I knew her father— he was the best and kindest friend I ever had."

"What!" exclaimed Thomas Nip. "You knew Gentleman Morris, the basket-maker?"

"Yes, well."

"And Miriam?"

"Yes, I have said so," exclaimed Dick, whose voice now trembled with an emotion he could not suppress. "I loved her, and I thought she loved me; but this night, when we met, she looked upon me with horror and disgust."

"And you are surprised?"

"I am—I feel, indeed, nearly broken-hearted."

The old man laughed a dry, cynical laugh.

"And did you suppose for a moment that, after she has been under the influence of Henry Dashwood, she would remain the same simple-hearted girl that *you* knew? No! dazzled by wealth she will fall an easy prey to the machinations of that villain; and— weak-minded as she is—will aid him willingly."

"Then *you* knew her," exclaimed Dick.

"Knew her?" cried Thomas Nip. "I see we do not quite understand one another yet. Before long I will tell you the real history of Gentleman Morris; and you will know then the terrible game which Henry Dashwood is playing. But, let me see, I have promised to reward you. Come to me tomorrow morning, at the office of Messrs.

Greed and Tact, Minding-lane, City, and I'll see what can be done for you. Meanwhile, here is a half-sovereign. Be off with you now, or my son Dion will be prying about the place."

Within a few minutes, Dick the Diver, after thanking his new employer, was once more floating on the river with his friend, the Joyful Haddock.

"How have you got on?" said the latter.

"First-rate," cried Dick. "I have got another half-sovereign. But look yonder, Joyful—there's a fire. See how red the sky is! Let's be off."

"How about our blow-out," said the Joyful Haddock, ruefully.

"Oh, we must put that off until to-morrow," said Dick; "don't let us lose the fun."

The fire, which had so naturally attracted the attention of Dick the Diver, was on the side of the river opposite to that on which Thomas Nip's house stood. And so, with a will, the boys crossed the stream, and ere long had landed at the stairs and moored their boat.

The red glow had now become more distinct; and, led by the glare, they ran up the steep river-side lane, and in less than a quarter of an hour they stood in front of Lennox's Country Hotel, where flames were pouring out through casements and roof.

An immense crowd was assembled; and the police had all their attention engaged in keeping the crowd back from the engines, which were puffing and snorting, and sending huge volumes of hissing water over the building.

There seemed to be an intense amount of excitement among the crowd, and to Dick's mind, practised as it was in matters of this kind, this seemed to suggest something important.

"Are all the people out?" he asked of a lad standing near.

"Don't know," was the answer. "There's been a-many strangers here to-night, so they say; and they rather fancy that they aint all out."

Dick's heart leaped at this idea.

"Come on, Joyful," he said; "perhaps there's a job for me here."

"You'd never go into that burning place?" cried the Joyful.

"Wouldn't I!" said Dick—"it wouldn't be the first time I've saved some one from fire."

As he spoke, and pressed forward to the front of the crowd, there was a sudden roar from a hundred throats; and then a swaying to and fro; and, looking up, the boys saw a white figure beckoning madly to the crowd.

In the glow and the smoke and the steam, no one could tell whether it was a man or a woman; but all knew that it was a human being in deadly peril, and their hearts beat high with fear and horror.

And yet not one was there in that crowd who volunteered to brave that barrier of fire.

There was a fire-escape standing up against the wall of the building, but some mishap had occurred to it; and now, through the crowd, came a man hurrying with a tall ladder, which swayed to and fro as it was hurriedly planted against the window where the frantic figure had appeared and disappeared.

The ladder was planted truly!

But still the mob hesitated—strong men yearning to go, and yet being kept back by some inner warning voice; weak women fainting, or hugging their babes to their heaving breasts, or clutching the arm of a father, a brother, a husband, or a lover, to save him from a sudden inspiration of human kindness.

But this awful suspense lasted but for an instant.

A young fireman was hurrying up, when Dick the Diver came springing along through the open space, and ran up the ladder with the speed and agility of a monkey.

A loud cheer resounded as he did so; and women's bosoms throbbed with a choking feeling of gratitude to the noble boy, and men felt angry with themselves that they had not so acted before.

Reaching the window, he dashed his foot through two panes of glass, kicked away a part of the woodwork, and then, amid the volume of smoke which rolled out, he sprang in and disappeared, amid the death-like silence which followed those ringing cheers.

Dick had heard nothing.

His heart was full of his brave purpose; and all he was conscious of was that a human being was in dire and terrible distress; and that, despite all his own hopes and purposes in life, he was bound to use for good the splendid courage with which Providence had endowed him.

On entering the room, he for a moment found himself enveloped in such a dense mass of smoke that he could see nothing.

A faint glimmer, as of a feeble light glowing amid the rest of the red glow, met his gaze after a moment, however; and he made towards it.

Then he soon discovered the state of affairs.

He was standing in a bed-room, the floor of which on one side was absolutely eaten away by the flames.

On the floor was extended the form of a female, insensible, and attired only in her night-dress.

Flying to her side, and kneeling down,

Dick found that she was a young girl, not more than seventeen years of age—beautiful, he could see, even in that moment.

"Wake, wake!" he cried, placing his hand upon her shoulder, and shaking her—"wake, wake!"

But not a sign of life was there.

Dick was a strong lad—of course, the life he had led since childhood was such as to nerve his muscles and enlarge his limbs—but to raise the young woman, and bear her away unassisted, seemed truly beyond his power.

However, he raised her in his arms as well as he could, and faced the wall of fire and flame, which was now fast spreading to the side of the room which contained the window.

He glanced at it a moment, and then made a dash forward.

His head grew dizzy, the smoke appeared as if it would choke him, and he was almost losing consciousness, when a voice at the window spoke.

"Hurry on—I'm here."

It was the voice of the Joyful Haddock.

He had not truly ventured to pass into that glowing mass of fire; but he was there, near at hand, to give his help.

Still clutching firmly the insensible body of the young girl, Dick staggered to the casement, and with the assistance of his friend got on the ladder and descended.

How he did so he never knew. All he was conscious of was that he came down with a run, and was received in the arms of an excited, swaying, shouting crowd.

When he awoke to consciousness he was lying on a sofa in a handsome room, with a gentleman and lady sitting by him, and watching him anxiously; while in an arm-chair, near a glowing fire, sat—fully dressed now, and looking very pale, but very beautiful—the young girl he had saved.

It was Alice Daly.

Another link in the strange chain of mystery was forged!

---

## CHAPTER XVI.

### BRIGHT PROSPECTS.

RS. DALY bent over Dick as he attempted to rise, and said—

"Don't try to get up, my lad. Drink this glass of wine—you must feel faint and ill."

So Dick indeed did; and, as he attempted to move, he knew by the acute pain in his arm that he had been burned severely.

His arm was covered with bandages, and he felt truly as if no power was left in his body.

As he drank the wine, Alice rose, and advancing with a sweet blush, took his hand.

"Brave lad," she said, "to you I owe my life."

"Yes," said Mrs. Daly, "we owe to you the life of our only child."

"And," added Mr. Daly, "you need do nothing now but try to get well. We shall see after your interests."

Dick, however, was not one of the weak order of beings.

The glass of wine had revived him so much, that in spite of the pain of his arm, he sat up, gazing in a kind of delighted wonder at the face of the beautiful girl he had saved—a face utterly different to that of Miriam Morris, but still one that could be loved equally with hers.

"I am grateful for your thanks, sir," he said, turning to Mr. Daly. "You could not reward me better than by procuring for me some permanent employment. I have some promised me; but it is, I fancy, of a kind not in any way suited to me."

Poor Augustus Daly!

In the fulness of his heart, and his gratitude to Dick the Diver for his brave conduct, he forgot that he himself was in search of some one to look after *his* interest, and was not even in a position to give the boy a sovereign.

"You shall have employment," repeated Mrs. Daly. "I have no doubt, Augustus, Mrs. Dashwood—why, what is the matter, my boy, are you ill?"

The boy had started and turned pale as the name of Dashwood was mentioned.

But yet he had the sense not to betray himself.

"I feel a severe twinge of pain," he said, as he rose. "I think I would rather go home now. I am very much obliged to you for your kindness.

"Don't mention such a thing," said Daly, with a smile. "Do we not owe to you the life of this our only daughter? If you *will* go home, let it be so for to-night, and I will get a cab for you; but let us see you in the morning."

"I will come, sir," replied Dick; "but I don't know where I am."

"No. 14, Armor-street, Bishopsgate. Ask for Mr. Daly."

"And if you please, sir, where is my friend—he that helped me down the ladder with the young lady?"

Mr. Daly laughed.

"Oh!" he said, "he that said his name was the Joyful Haddock. He went home, refusing all presents, and said he'd rather leave you in good hands!"

As Dick reached the door, Alice Daly ran up to him, and seized his hand.

"I shall never, never forget you," she said, in a voice tremulous with emotion; "you are a brave, generous boy, and your face tells me that you are as good as you are brave!"

And with this assurance from her lips, he went away with an idea that, perhaps, after all, there was one being in the world as good and as beautiful as Miriam Morris.

In his dreamy reverie, as he walked along, he forgot all about his wounded arm; but presently, as he found himself nearing London Bridge, the keen air reminded him. And now, at the approach of morning—the chill hours when the dying mostly reach their last hour—he turned sick and faint, and he resolved not to go to Rotherhithe.

It was a long and weary walk, and not caring to spend any more money in cabs, he took a bed in the City, where he could be close by the office of Greed and Tact, those two worthy members of the Secret Seven.

Twelve next day found him sitting in the outer office of the agents, waiting for Thomas Nip.

To and fro came the clients—some jaunty and merry, others dejected and careworn; some entering with cheerful smiles and departing with looks of hungry despair; others coming bowed down with grief, and issuing forth with a joyous and eager excitement.

Presently the office boy came out, and said, in a squeaky voice—

"Come in, Mr. Nip can just spare you two minutes."

Had Dick been unfortunate enough to make his appearance at the office in his diving clothes, he would have been the source of unnatural excitement and wonder to this boy, who imagined himself a connoisseur in dress.

Our hero, however, had taken the precaution to attire himself in a brand-new suit from some City clothier's; so, having no fault to find, the young Cerberus quickly admitted him to the presence of Mr. Thomas Nip, whom he found with his nose deep in a huge box of snuff.

"Ah! come in, lad, come in," cried Nip, off-handedly; then he added, as the other boy left the room—"I'm obliged to be particular what I say here. You see, I'm not the master, by no means, you see. But now, come here. It's rather a curious business I wish to employ you on, and we must be secret."

He gave him a chair close to where he himself was sitting, by his high desk, and then went on—

"I see you've got better clothes, that's one good thing. What I want you to do is to watch this Henry Dashwood, day and night, if you think you can. He'll be nearly always moving about in the day and the night, and it'll be some trouble; but I'll pay you well. Now, this very day I expect him to go down to the river-side, near Wapping somewhere. I want him watched, and if you'll do it, you shall have another half-sovereign."

Dick the Diver thought at once of Augustus Daly.

He had promised to call there: it would be ungrateful not to do so, and against his own interests, moreover.

And then, again, there was Alice Daly!

"At what time do you want me to start?" he asked.

At this instant the door opened, and the office boy said—

"Mr. Nip, Mr. Henry Dashwood wishes to see you."

"He follows me everywhere," said Dick. But Nip did not hear him.

"Quick," he cried, "get into yonder cupboard. You'll hear all we say; and perhaps it may be for your interest and mine."

Dick lost no time in following Nip's advice, and, as the closet door closed behind him, Henry Dashwood entered.

---

## CHAPTER XVII.

### WHAT DICK HEARD IN THE CUPBOARD, AND THE RESULT.

 "GOOD morning, Mr. Dashwood," cried Nip, cheerily, rubbing his hands. "Quite an unexpected pleasure."

"Ah! just so," said Dashwood, not even hearing the old clerk's remark, "just so. The truth is I came to see either Mr. Greed or Mr. Tact, and I find that neither of them is expected till the afternoon."

"Quite so," said Mr. Nip, and rubbed his hands harder.

"You see," pursued Dashwood, as he took a seat near the old man's desk—"you see, I wish to make a good offer to Messrs. Greed and Tact in reference to my friend Augustus Daly. You know the name?"

"Quite well. He it was that we turned out of Brown's house by forfeiture of bill of sale."

"Just so," said Dashwood. "Of course you, as one of the Secret Seven, know our way of business. Now, I want to get Daly a Government appointment, or something. I want to place him under an obligation to me, some way. Of course, he knows nothing of me under my present name; in fact, I have my reasons for desiring he should not. However, I have lent him the money to settle this matter with; and of course, as I know Greed and Tact are the very best for him to employ, I thought it might as well not go out of the firm."

Thomas Nip laughed, and placed one forefinger on the other by way of strengthening the argument.

"If Mr. Daly wishes the thing done, he couldn't come to a better place," he said. "You are clever, Mr. Dashwood, very clever."

And he smiled, so that if Dick—whose head was now peeping from the cupboard—had not known that Nip was aware of his listening, he would have believed him a traitor.

"Nip," said Dashwood, "you are a clever fellow, too; but don't run into compliments—you know I never like them. Tell Greed and Tact, if Daly calls here, to promise him anything; and say, also, that I wish them really to assist him to a berth. It will be something off my mind, and will, moreover, aid me in a design I have—a design which must be accomplished."

"Very well," said Mr. Nip, drawing, as it were, within himself, when he found he had displeased his visitor by his show of praise, "I will do as you desire. Is there anything else you want at present?"

"Well, it is almost needless to ask," replied Dashwood, in a voice of irritation, "have you heard any tidings of that infernal young scoundrel whom they call Dick the Diver? I have searched every way—in Daddy Spindle's kitchen, and every back slum and evil haunt I can imagine, but without effect."

Dick now listened more intently, and his heart, as may be imagined, went pit-a-pat, as he heard his name mentioned in this manner.

What could it mean?

It was hardly possible that these two men were leagued together against him.

"So have I," said Thomas Nip, "but I hadn't such a chance as *you* had. The truth is that I had such a meagre description of him that I could not describe him. Had I caught the young villain, I would have delivered him over at once; but you surely have better fish to catch than a river boy? Have you found the Lascar yet?"

Henry Dashwood glanced round as if he were afraid that, in very truth, walls had ears.

"Be careful," he said, "you don't know who may be listening. No, I have not found the Lascar; but at eight to-night I am going to Tiger Bay, and there I am almost certain to find him. I go to the Turtle and Pig at eight, and—unless his pal has deceived me instead of splitting on him—I shall know the whole story."

"You are not then satisfied yet?" said Thomas Nip.

"As to what?"

"As to whether that was really Mark Ashton who was murdered on the seventh of November on board the *Valparaiso*."

"I *am* satisfied."

"Why, then, are you so anxious to know more?"

"Because my satisfaction is a *dissatisfaction*," said Henry Dashwood. "My belief is that it was *not* Mark Ashton, and I want to prove that it was."

Thomas Nip rubbed his hands again.

Rubbed them in such a way that it almost seemed to Dick Ashton that it was with pleasure at what he was discovering rather than at anything else.

"Just so," he said—"just so. I understand you perfectly. It might, in fact, be awkward if it was found that it was *not* Mark Ashton. Is this Lascar trustworthy?"

"Yes," said Henry Dashwood, with a strange smile, and a gloomy cloud passed over his features, while he remained in utter silence.

Then he rose suddenly.

"Well, you understand me, Nip," he added, as he prepared to go. "You will explain to Greed and Tact what I want. I fancy Daly will be here to-day. Good morning."

And so he went.

Nip left his seat, and tiptoed up against the glass partition until he saw him well out of the place; then he approached the cupboard, saying—

"Now then, Dick, you can come out."

Dick issued forth, flushed and excited.

"Did you hear all?" asked Nip.

"Every word."

"Now, you see your enemy," replied the clerk; "but remember *I* am your friend, and not one word of anything you have seen or heard must be repeated to any one. You and I together are at present enough to defeat him."

"Not one word of all this shall pass my lips," said Dick. "I *know* him to be my enemy, and my object is to catch him tripping. But I know Mr. Daly."

"You do?" cried Thomas Nip, in surprise.

"Yes," said Dick, "it was through him and his that I got my arm in a sling like this." And then circumstantially he narrated the events of the night before, the fire, the saving of Alice, and the promises held forth by Augustus Daly.

Thomas Nip considered awhile, as if about to make some further revelation.

But then he drew himself up, muttering to himself—

"No—no, I won't just now," and said, "Do you know Tiger Bay?"

"Well, I've heard of it," cried Dick, with a comic twinkle in his eye.

"Are you afraid to go there? I know it's a dangerous place."

"Not for such as I am," said the Diver. "It might be for Henry Dashwood, unless he knows his way about pretty well and has friends; but for me and my pals there couldn't be any harm."

"Very well," pursued the clerk; "I want you to follow Dashwood to-night to the Turtle and Pig, in Tiger Bay. He is going there at eight o'clock to-night to see a Lascar, who I believe knew Mark Ashton; and can either give good information respecting him, or can swear to something, which will be as good to Dashwood. I want to know all they do and all they say."

"Good," said Dick, "I'll go."

"You're a brave lad and will do well," said old Nip, rubbing his hands and looking strangely into the boy's face—"yes, better than you dream of yourself, much better. And you'll surprise Henry Dashwood ere long, I can promise you. Meanwhile, here is some more money. Be prudent with it, and don't get showing it too profusely in Tiger Bay. Be off now, for fear Greed and Tact should come in and see you."

"And when am I to come to you again?" asked Dick, pocketing the half-sovereign.

"To-night, after all is over, and by the window," said Nip. "I shall see that everything is quiet."

## CHAPTER XVIII.

### TIGER BAY.

EVERY one who is at all acquainted with the purlieus of the river knows Tiger Bay.

It lies just behind Ratcliffe Highway, and is frequented by the most abominable set of human beings that can possibly be imagined: women of loose character, foreign sailors, black men who have lost their certificates through crimes. And at night time, if you can imagine the public-houses doing a roaring trade, lights gleaming across the rudely paved streets, all in comparative darkness—save these palaces of drink—and a crowd of men and women and boys and girls shouting, swearing, singing, dancing, or reeling to and fro in helpless intoxication—if you can imagine this, you have some faint conception of the place.

It was towards this spot that Henry Dashwood was bound on the evening of his interview with Thomas Nip.

As may be imagined, he did not proceed thither in his usual costume; and if Dick the Diver had not been quick of apprehension, he would certainly have had to count his pursuit of his enemy among his failures.

But Dick was, as the Joyful Haddock expressed it, "up to snuff."

So, long before eight o'clock, Dick posted himself near the house in Park-lane, whither he had tracked Dashwood; and as the hour approached, he came closer in the darkness.

In order that his enemy might not recognise him, he had dressed himself in a borrowed suit of sailor's clothes, and darkened his skin; and so when Dashwood issued forth into the street and glanced around him, he took no notice whatever of the man-o'-war's lad who was lounging along with a regular sea roll.

Dashwood himself was attired in a reefing jacket, blue trousers, and a navy cap, while bushy false whiskers almost entirely concealed the character of his face.

But Dick knew his eyes; and quite confident that he was on the right track, he followed hastily in his wake.

Presently, Dashwood entered a cab, and the old game was repeated.

Dick entered another, and being ordered to keep the other one in view, they started off almost together.

At length the precincts of Tiger Bay were reached, and they discharged their cabs simultaneously.

Then Dashwood, without even a glance round, and never dreaming that he was pursued, darted down a dark alley, and went at a rapid trot over the rough stones.

This was the point where Dick was in greatest danger of being discovered—for at present, with the exception of the two, there was no one about.

But in a second the scene changed, and Dick had all his work to do to keep his quarry in sight, for there was suddenly a blaze of light, and a hurrying, bustling crowd which seemed scarcely to know which way it desired to move.

Among this Dashwood made his way with the familiarity of an old acquaintance; and presently, diving down another narrow alley, he emerged into a scene of greater bustle and excitement still.

But Dick the Diver never once lost sight of him.

Actuated by his own desire to punish Dashwood for the insults he had put upon him, he was also fired now by the same feeling which always animates a detective engaged in an exciting chase; and he would have been bitterly disappointed had he lost him, and been compelled to return without any news for Thomas Nip.

After a moment Dashwood entered the Turtle and Pig, and proceeding to the bar ordered some grog, which was soon steaming on the counter.

Dick, entering also, rolled up to the counter

and called for brandy; and his enemy, looking straight into his face, never even once suspected him.

Indeed, he was, in the first place, too much absorbed in his search for the Lascar; and, in the second place, there was nothing unusual in a man-of-war's lad being in Tiger Bay.

Presently a tall darkie entered the gin-shop.

He was attired in the ordinary dress of a Lascar, but his face was one which, once seen, could not easily be forgotten.

In fact, he was not quite a fair specimen of his race.

His eyes were large, mild, and had in them the fire of courage and generosity; his nose was straight, and his mouth supple and well shaped.

Dashwood glanced at him an instant, and then advanced, saying—

"Good evening, Hasib; can I speak with you?"

The Lascar looked searchingly into his face, and then replied with a strange smile, and in good English—

"Certainly, the gentleman can speak to me."

"In private, then," said Dashwood, and at once led the way into an inner room.

The door of this was then closed, and Dick the Diver was left to his brandy and his rough companions.

"What's to be done now?" thought he. "I can't enter that room; how, then, can I hear their conversation?"

He was thinking thus, when a hand was placed heavily upon his shoulder.

"Where do you hail from, mate?" cried a voice.

A voice he knew not.

Dick turned, and saw standing beside him a sailor, with a smiling and yet sinister face —apparently the face of a man who tried to cover his evil purposes under the cloak of merriment.

"Where do you hail from, mate?" he said again, diving his hands deep into his trousers pockets.

"By the *Fricasseed Balloon*, from the Ham and Beef Islands," cried Dick, with a laugh, which was joined in by those present.

The man looked savage.

"I shall pull your ear, youngster," he said, "if you tackle me with any of your cheek— so you'd best sheer off."

"Another glass of grog, landlord," said Dick, without taking any notice of the man's injunction.

The man looked as it were aghast at the boy's impudence.

Then he rolled off to where two other men were standing.

"That's the lad," he said. "I know him by his eyes and by his impudence. He's a regular cheeky one, and 'll make a fine sailor."

Dick, finding the man said no more, and not wanting the grog in reality, went up to him, and offered him the glass, saying—

"Here, shipmate, take a drink. I've been to Shark Island, and know the ways of the animals. They're very vicious, but a piece of pig makes them always civil."

This allusion to the name of the house caused another laugh, and the treacherous sailor held out his hand.

"Give us a grip, youngster," he said; "you have got the gift of the gab, but I like a chap as can give an answer when he is required. I'll drink with you with pleasure."

"Drink hearty, shipmate," said Dick; "I've had enough."

And with these words he sauntered towards the door.

"Look out, Ned," said one of the sailors; "he is off."

"Never mind," said the other; "the ship doesn't sail for a week, and I always know where to put my hand upon him when I want him."

"That is all very well," said the other sailor. "What, in the name of squalls, did he want down here?"

"Hallo! youngster, from the Ham and Beef Islands," cried the man who had first spoken, "you are out of your latitude, aint you? What are you doing down this way?"

"I am like you," cried Dick the Diver— "I am looking out for flats, and can't find them."

And then, amidst a burst of merriment, in which he himself joined, Dick hastened from the gin palace.

In spite, however, of his laughter, our hero knew well that something sinister was hidden beneath this simple incident; and as he passed into the street, he looked anxiously behind him to see if he were followed.

Even this feeling, however, was driven from his mind by a sight which met his eyes.

Henry Dashwood and the Lascar had, truly, concealed themselves in a private room, but they had forgotten to close the window.

This window was not facing the street, but looked out upon a bye-way, in which not a human being was visible.

In an instant Dick the Diver had glided down the dark avenue, and crouched down near the casement.

And this is what he heard.

"Well, Hasib," said Dashwood, "you know how I became acquainted with your existence, and that I shall give you a good reward for any service you may afford me?"

"Yes," said the Lascar, quietly.

DICK RESCUES ALICE DALY FROM THE FLAMES.

"Well, then, in the first place, you came to England on board the *Valparaiso?*"

"I did."

"And there was a Mark Ashton on board?"

"No, there was not."

Both Henry Dashwood and Dick the Diver started at this quiet intimation.

"But there *was*," said Henry Dashwood, with a kind of dogged annoyance. "He came from New York. He reached the Pool, somehow or another he fell into bad company, was robbed and murdered; and his body, being recovered, was found to have the letters 'M. A.' tattooed upon his breast. He was buried, and in the night some one scrawled on his headstone the name of 'Mark Ashton.'"

"Any one, even you, might have done that," said the Lascar, with a quiet smile: "but as to the tattooing, that means nothing. It might have been Mark Arnold, or Matthew Anstey, or any such name."

"Who, then, was this man who was murdered in the Thames?" asked Henry Dashwood, eagerly. "He must have been a friend of Mark Ashton, for the papers found on him prove it."

"His name was Mark Arundel," said the Lascar. "Mark Ashton lives to avenge him."

The stern and solemn way in which these words were spoken made Harry Dashwood start and turn pale, and sent a thrill through every pulse in Dick the Diver's body.

The mystery was now revealing itself with a vengeance.

For a few moments there was complete silence.

At length, Dashwood said—

"I am glad to hear it. It was a cruel and cowardly murder, and it is the place of Mark Ashton to punish the murderer of his friend. But come, let us leave this place. The papers, as I have told you, are in the custody of a man who lives across the water. They will explain, better than I can, the reason of my suspicions."

The two men then drank up their grog, and proceeded towards the river-side.

---

## CHAPTER XIX.

### A DIVE FOR LIFE.

 BRIGHT moonlight was streaming over the Thames when Hasib the Lascar and Henry Dashwood put off from the shore.

All was as still as death, and the shadows of the big ships lay upon a lake-like river, reflecting the great moon, which hung like a gigantic lamp in the sky, as it had done on the night of the murder of the passenger from New York.

The Lascar sat at the stern of the boat, while Henry Dashwood took the oars and began to pull vigorously in the direction of the Rotherhithe shore.

Dick the Diver had glided along thus far unperceived; but now came the difficulty.

The moonlight was so bright, it was quite impossible for him to enter a boat and pull after them unperceived.

What was to be done?

The pursuit was too good to be abandoned; and, besides, there was a dread presentiment in his mind that something evil was intended.

He looked about him eagerly.

Boats there were in plenty; but as this was an absurdity on such a bright night, he abandoned the idea of them altogether.

Suddenly an idea struck him.

There was a large barge drawn up close to the shore, and three more lying at different distances from one another, while connecting each was a plank.

Rushing through the water up to his knees, Dick clambered up into the first barge, and running quickly across this entered the second, and so on to the end.

Then, regardless of the law of property, but knowing full well that he should return the boat, he jumped into a skiff and pulled away after the other one, which had now taken mid-stream and was proceeding down towards Greenwich.

Henry and the Lascar were not observing him.

In fact, the idea of another boat being on the river at that early hour was nothing, and so there was nothing to suspect.

On reaching the side of a large brig, which lay like a sullen monster on the bosom of the river, Henry Dashwood purposely lost an oar.

"Halloa! here's an accident," he cried. "Bother it! See if there's another one down there."

Hasib unsuspectingly moved forward and sought for the oar.

In an instant Henry Dashwood was upon him.

"Wretch!" he cried—"wretch! your last hour has come."

It is strange that murderers, as a rule, address words to their victims as if they were really desirous of putting them on their guard.

But the Lascar, in spite of the words, which he perfectly comprehended, had no time to avoid the hands which grappled with his throat.

He was strong and lithe, however, and in an instant a deadly struggle began within the little craft.

Henry Dashwood was so furiously determined to effect his deadly purpose, that he never for an instant paused to think where the boat was drifting.

It circled round in the water, which was now gradually beginning to ebb, and once and again bumped against obstacles.

But never for a moment remembering the huge steam monsters which could have run them down in an instant, Henry Dashwood struggled with his resolute adversary.

Presently a voice came.

"Halloa, what's the matter there?"

Even at that terrible moment, Henry Dashwood knew that voice.

Knew it, and trembled.

He made no answer.

Only his hands clenched tighter round the neck of his victim, and he raised him to the edge of the boat, while Dick, divining that something was the matter—though he could not see which was the aggressor—pulled fiercely on behind.

Suddenly, just as Henry Dashwood imagined that he had settled his hideous scheme at last, there came a terrific swell, and the lurch of the boat flung Dashwood off his knees.

The Lascar was now uppermost, and the intending murderer saw by the deadly gleam in his eyes that his own life, if not well protected, would fall a sacrifice to the vengeance of the infuriated black.

But his blood was not only up, but he was given a supernatural kind of strength by the fear of death.

Again they fought, and again Henry Dashwood was uppermost.

And then, just as Dick the Diver had nearly reached the boat, the Indian gasped convulsively—his neck seized by the infuriated grasp of his would-be murderer in a still tighter grip—uttered a startling cry, and over he went into the bubbling water.

Dick the Diver at that moment came up to the spot, and for an instant hesitated what to do.

Was he to save the drowning man, whose black face and gleaming eyes he had seen disappear beneath the waves, or was he first to punish the murderer?

Chance decided for him.

He saw the dark figure of the Lascar sinking beneath the waves, and with a natural spirit of humanity he rowed swiftly towards the spot.

The Lascar had received such a terrific blow at the last moment, and had, moreover, been so nearly strangled, that his strength was nearly gone when he went beneath the water; so that after one gasping cry, and a bubbling attempt at speech, he sank.

But the deliverer was near.

With fury concentrated in his heart, Dashwood saw Dick the Diver approach the spot, pulling hard with his oars, while he himself had none.

Then he beheld the boy throw his jacket into the boat, and take one long deliberate dive beneath the waves.

He was seeking for treasure again, but this time the treasure was a human life.

It was a daring and an almost desperate action, for the dark body of the unfortunate man was of course hardly to be distinguished from the black water round it.

But Dick's experience taught him what to do, and underneath the waves of old Father Thames he struck out, till presently rising he saw once more the form of the wretched Indian.

"He is not dead," thought Dick. "No, no—he wouldn't come up now if he were."

Away swam the gallant boy in the direction of the body.

It was an exciting moment.

Fired with insane rage, and reckless now as to discovery, Henry Dashwood, knowing full well that he would have two witnesses against him, strove with efforts that seemed superhuman to reach them by means of his one oar.

But in vain.

Dick's strong arm had now encircled the body of the Indian, and he was swimming away with him to the shore.

---

## CHAPTER XX.

### VENGEANCE BETTER THAN DEATH.

ERY nearly exhausted by his exertions, Dick, when he reached the bank, would have dropped his burden once more into the water had not a friendly hand been extended to him.

A voice, too, spoke to him in a familiar tone.

"Hallo! what's up, Dick—another body?"

It was the voice of the Joyful Haddock.

"I hope it aint a body," cried Dick, as well as he could speak for the filthy water, which had nearly choked him. "I fancy he's a lively one. Help us up further."

The two boys together soon contrived to raise the body of the Lascar into the narrow street, where a gleaming light showed the proximity of one of those houses of entertainment which abound in that locality.

"Run him along here, to the Bull and Magpie," said the Joyful Haddock. "Oh, my, he's a black un!"

"Yes, and a good one as well," said Dick the Diver—"a faithful and true friend; and I hope I'll save him. Here we are, run him in."

"That's all very well," said the Joyful Haddock, "but money—"

"Bother that!" cried Dick; "he'll die out here, if we waste time talking. Civility can be bought, if it doesn't exist. Come on."

Amid an excited throng which crowded the bar, the two boys carried the still insensible man into a warm room, where, at their earnest request—and in consequence, may be, of the display of some money which Dick made—he was seen to at once.

It was soon discovered that he was not dead.

His limbs lost their stiffness, his eyes opened, and presently he glared round him with a wild stare.

He comprehended all, as it seemed, in a moment, and pressed his hand to his brow.

"Ah!" he cried, "I remember all now—all, all! The villain!"

"Yes," said Dick, "I know him well, and I—"

The Lascar placed his finger on his lip.

"I would not injure him," he said, in a low whisper, that only Dick could hear—"no, no! I know a vengeance for him worse than death!"

Dick the Diver did not comprehend the words then, but he thought of them, and shuddered at them, a long time after.

He was able soon by restoratives to sit up, and he asked to be left alone awhile with Dick.

## CHAPTER XXI.

### DICK IS ENTRUSTED WITH A SECRET.

WHEN every one had left the room except Dick and the Lascar, the latter said—

"Do you know this Dashwood?"

"I do, well," replied Dick—"he is a wicked and bitter-hearted man. I can swear, and I will swear, that he tried to take your life this night."

The Lascar, Hasib, smiled.

"No—no," he answered, "no—no! You forget my late words. I do not wish that he should be punished by the law. I will be the one to punish him. Where does he live?"

"In Park-lane, No. 16."

"Very good—very good," said the Lascar. "I will go to see him."

"But is your life safe with him?"

"Yes, in the daylight. I fear him not! Yes—yes, I will see him," said the Lascar; "and now, boy, as you have saved my life, I owe you a reward."

"No, no," said Dick, "you owe me none for doing my duty."

"It is a strange reward, my lad," pursued Hasib, "not of the kind you mean. I would not insult you by offering you money, had I it to give, which I have not. No, my answer to your kind work for me this night is—keep for me a secret."

"I will, indeed, upon my sacred honour," said Dick, impressed strangely by the man's manner.

The Lascar leaned forward and lowered his voice.

"Boy," he cried, "it is impossible in life to know what may become of one; and so, though I have been this night miraculously preserved, who knows but that I may die to-morrow? Therefore take this packet of papers. If at the end of two years I do not return, believe that I am dead; open them, and make use of them; but believe me, if Heaven preserves my life, I will be here on the 1st of January, 1869, to open them with you and punish my enemies."

"But if, while you are absent, he dies?" suggested Dick, as he placed the papers in his pocket.

The Lascar pointed upwards.

"I trust in the goodness of Heaven," he said—"it will save him for my vengeance. Now we will part; and, as you respect and honour justice, betray me not."

"Never," said Dick, and grasped the Lascar's hand—"I swear it!"

Then they parted, and Dick and the Joyful Haddock were soon rowing over the river.

"A boat and a coat gone, Joyful," cried Dick; "but I've won a secret, and I think it is one worth having."

"You're always discovering some kind of treasure," said the Joyful Haddock. "What is it now? It can't be much out of a nigger."

"Oh, yes, it is, Joyful; but I am bound not to tell it," replied Dick. "I can't break my word."

"I don't ask you," replied the Joyful. "I wouldn't have you break your word for the world. Where are you going to-night?"

"To Daddy Spindle's."

"What, there! and when you've got coin?"

"Yes, I must save it," said Dick. "I don't know what I may have to do with it. I'm going to Daddy's to see the poor old chap that we saved from the river, when his senses were gone. I believe, though, I don't know why, that he has some connection with this horrid mystery in which I have been mixed up."

The boys, having rowed themselves across without seeing anything of Henry Dashwood, soon found themselves within the shelter of old Spindle's establishment.

After supper Dick made his way up into the room where the old man lay.

The old man, tired out with his long watching, had fallen asleep.

Dick's candle burnt low and expired. Then he also fell into a sound slumber.

Suddenly he awoke.

A slight sound had disturbed him.

On opening his eyes, he saw a man creep glidingly to the side of the bed on which the seaman slept.

The old sailor—a light sleeper, and more light now than ever—immediately sprang up.

In the bright moonlight he saw the face of his would-be murderer.

In an instant he recognized the midnight visitor.

Then with a wild cry of "Fred!—Fred Armor!" he sank back.

"Fool!" muttered the murderer, lifting aloft his knife.

But it did not descend.

Dick sprang across the room, and heeding not the difference in their size and age, grappled fiercely with the villain.

The man turned fiercely on Dick; a heavy blow was struck, and, unable to resist the iron strength of the man, the Diver fell stunned to the floor.

He was at last in the power of his foe!

## CHAPTER XXII.

### A STRUGGLE IN THE DARK.

ICK the Diver was never nearer death than when, on that night, in Daddy Spindle's upper room, he lay at the mercy of the murderer of the supposed Mark Ashton.

He was nearly insensible, and though he could just have strength to move and raise his hand to ward off a second blow, he was powerless to struggle.

"Ha, ha! my youngster," he cried, forgetful that his voice could be heard—"ha, ha! I have you now, and nothing can save you."

"That's just where you make a mistake," cried a voice at this instant.

And then, with one bound, the Joyful Haddock sprang upon the back of his neck, giving it a feeling as if it were dislocated.

Then he commenced an onslaught upon the villain's head, banging him right and left, before he sprang up and overturned him.

The knife had dropped from his grasp as he rose, and the Joyful Haddock at once seized it.

"I'll murder you," said the ruffian, as he staggered back, and pushed the hair from off his eyes.

"I'm afraid it'll be the other way if you don't keep off," cried the Joyful Haddock. "I've got the knife here, and if you come any of your tricks, I'll stick you."

But the ruffian was blinded to danger by his rage, and with a yell of fury he rushed upon the boy.

"I'll be the death of you?" cried he.

But the Joyful Haddock was too much for him.

Whirling his long knife round, he brought it down with such a vengeance that it penetrated his assailant's arm.

The murderer sprang back with a loud cry of rage and pain, and, by the flash that followed, Dick the Diver knew at once that he had drawn a revolver.

This was, of course, instant death to some one.

So Dick knew well that it was neck or nothing; and seeing the danger in which his friend stood, he chanced everything, and dashed upon the villain.

The murderer of Mark Ashton—or, as the Lascar called him, Mark Arundel—was, however, a strong man, and the boys would have had no chance with him.

Dick bravely seized him by the wrist, and held it firmly; but he was as a baby in the hands of a giant, and was gradually being forced down upon his knees, when another person appeared upon the scene.

This was Bully Wrench.

His burly figure hesitated an instant in the doorway, and then, with an ejaculation which is scarcely polite enough to place in print, he dashed upon the murderer.

The boys saw him in the moonlight, and dropped just at the moment when the new-comer came to the rescue, so that in the scurry the pistol fell to the ground.

Bully Wrench had him in his stalwart arms before he was well aware that any one was present.

"Why, bash my head with a tombstone!" he cried, "if I aint a good mind to throttle you right off. Come into the moonlight, and let us have a look at you."

The murderer of Mark Arundel, powerless in the hands of his new enemy, suffered himself to be dragged to the opening which served as a window, and there Bully Wrench held him, while the strong light fell upon his features.

"Darn my buttons!" cried he, "you are a stranger anyhow, and a devilish ugly-looking one. What brings you here?"

At this instant, before the murderer could reply, a faint voice was heard from the bed.

"Am I mad, am I mad?"—it was the old man that was speaking—"or am I on board the *Valparaiso* once more?"

"Do you know the villain?" cried Bully Wrench.

But it was of no avail to speak.

The old man had relapsed once more into unconsciousness, and, in spite of the efforts of Dick the Diver and the Joyful Haddock, not another word could be extracted from him.

"Well, darn me!" said Bully Wrench, addressing the now trembling man—"darn me! if we want you here. The nearest way out is by the window; so out you go."

The man muttered a curse, but, in the arms of Bully Wrench, he was entirely helpless.

Struggling in every way, kicking, plunging, and striking, the murderer was raised in the giant arms of Bully Wrench, until he reached the level of the window.

Then the resolute man paused an instant, as if to recover strength to carry out his determination; and suddenly, with a resolute swing, he dashed the murderer through the open casement.

All waited an instant, until a heavy splash below told that he had entered the river.

"He's met water fine," said Wrench, with a smile. "Strikes me he won't come around here again for some time."

Dick the Diver was looking eagerly for his appearance on the surface of the moonlit river.

"I hope you haven't killed him," said he, as he peered about in vain for him.

"Why should he live?" asked Bully Wrench; "he's a murderer—or, at least, he meant to be; he was going to do for one or both of you."

"Yes," said Dick, "but his life holds a secret. If he dies, so does a mystery which may mean more than gold to *me*."

"Well, then," laughed Wrench, "I think I see his head bobbing up and down like a cork yonder;—dive for him."

"It is needless, he is swimming," said Dick; "let him go. When I want him I know where to find him. *I* am going to punish the one who set him on to this night's work. *Him* I leave to the vengeance of Heaven."

"I say, Dick," cried Bully Wrench, "you've seen to some of these 'ere penny plays I think, or you wouldn't be after talking like *that*. However, if there's anything the matter, and you want the help of Tom Wrench's arm, there it is; it's got a slight muscle, my lad, and there's a heart behind it somewhere, only I aint had much use for it."

"Thank you, Tom," cried Dick; "and now let's see to the old man."

---

## CHAPTER XXIII.

### FACE TO FACE.

ARK LANE was immersed in darkness.

The inhabitants of most of the houses had gone either to the theatre or the ball, and every-thing was very still when Dick the Diver knocked at the door of No. 17.

He had resolved to face his fate.

Not as regards Miriam.

Of her, he, in fact, endeavoured not to think—the past seemed so utterly blotted out as regarded her; the old days appeared so entirely a thing of memory, that he scarcely wished to think of her; but with Henry Dashwood he was resolved to have a reckoning.

"Is Mr. Dashwood at home?" he asked, boldly, as he brought the servant to the door by a loud summons.

"No, he is not; but he will not be long," said the servant, eyeing him somewhat askance.

"May I wait?"

"Yes—come into the hall."

Had James the butler been the one who had opened to him, it might have been a different affair—that pompous functionary would most likely have shut the door in his face.

As it was, however, Deborah the house-maid had been born with a little of the milk of human kindness in her nature, and she naturally felt a sympathy with the lad.

So she placed him in a chair near the hall fire, stirred up the smouldering embers, and left him not until she had administered to him the gentle stimulant of a glass of ale.

Sitting there by the fire in the servants' sanctum, strange thoughts flitted through the brain of Dick the Diver.

Why was he there?

Why was it, too, that he who had been brought up to believe himself a mudlark, who had sought his living in the depths of the river, who had been compelled by fate to associate with the lowest of the low—why was it that his heart revolted from the idea of being placed there in the hall to wait the good time of such a wretch as Henry Dashwood?

He was wondering himself at this, when his eyes suddenly encountered a vision which brought the rich blood in torrents to his face, and brought, too, the memory back of all the old days—happy now they seemed to him compared with the present.

It was Miriam!

She was dressed all in white, with her beautiful shoulders bare and gleaming, a diamond cross resting upon her bosom, flowers in her hair, rings on her dimpled fingers.

A vision above him—a vision of loveliness which he had only dreamt of, and which even crushed him, as it had done before on the night he had followed her to the Opera.

She did not see him.

In her hand was a book, and either in the remembrance of the contents of the volume, or in her thoughts of herself, she was so immersed that she never looked at anything, but sailed majestically into the drawing-room.

Poor Dick!

He had seen Alice Daly, he had felt a strange and thrilling sensation when she had held his hand and thanked him; but Miriam was the old love—the love of his poverty, the love of the boyhood which, amid direst misery, had seen brightness only at that quiet fireside with her and Gentleman Morris.

He couldn't stand that waiting there in the servants' hall, while she—the companion of those ever brightening hours—was, queen-like, sitting within in luxury, not even knowing of his presence.

So, rising up, and utterly regardless of etiquette or danger, he hurried into the drawing-room, rough and muddy as he was.

She was sitting on a *causée* near the elaborately decorated fireplace, her tiny slippered feet rested on a stool, her gleaming neck was cosily enveloped in a white fur boa, which she had just taken up; her golden hair lay lovingly upon her bare shoulders, the flush of health or excitement was on her cheeks, and her bright eyes were fixed upon vacancy.

He hurried forward.

" Miriam !"

It was all he could say.

But it had its immediate effect.

She started up. The light of her eyes fled away, the colour in her cheeks faded, the love and life of her whole being vanished and left a statue—a breathing, animated piece of stone, with utter scorn on its lips, hatred in its eyes, horror and selfish terror permeating it everywhere.

" You here !" she cried. " What means this unmerited insult ?"

And she moved towards the bell-rope.

He dashed between it and her.

" Beware, mad girl !" he cried, " beware ! I do not come to insult you. I did not even know that I should meet you. I came to see Mr. Henry Dashwood. As he is *not* here, I waited. I saw you, I knew you—and oh, Miriam ! the memory of the old times came back : the dear old evenings in that quiet room, where you knew no greater happiness than listening to your father's stories; when the whole reward of my wretched, toilsome existence was to sit at your feet and love you. Fear not, it is all gone. I see the light of the past shut out from your eyes. If I could recall it, it would only bring back what you have cast away as useless, and so it would bring no joy to me. I have met you before, and—"

Miriam stamped her foot upon the floor.

" Wretched boy !" she cried, with white lips, while her pale face and heaving bosom showed how great was her agitation. " What *can* you wish? The past by *me* is utterly forgotten, as it should be by you. I am in a different sphere of life. The misery which was once my lot has passed away, my father—whose madness kept me from wealth and comfort—is dead. I must live a new life. I do not wish to remember the horrid and useless past. Forget *me*, for I have forgotten you; and children as we are—though misfortune has tried to make us man and woman—let us think of a new life, in which, however, we meet no more."

Dick's eyes flashed fire.

" Let it be so," he said. " I will quit this place at once; but remember my words. From the time that my eyes first drank in the beauty of your presence, I loved you—I love you now; but I will tear you from my heart. Be happy, be rich, and fear no interruption from me in the course which you have marked out for yourself. Recollect, if ever you need a friend, that you have not, even by your bitter scorn, made an enemy of Richard Ashton !"

He turned to go, with the full design of quitting the place.

But her look detained him.

At the mention of the name she became more deadly white than ever. Her every limb trembled, and she staggered to the table for support.

" Richard Ashton !" she cried. " What mean you? Your name is not that."

A smile wreathed itself over Dick's lips, a swelling pride filled his breast, a resolute manliness came to him.

" Yes," he said calmly, " my name is Richard Ashton; and, as far as my knowledge goes, I am the son of the wretched man who was murdered on board the ship *Valparaiso* by a friend of Mr. Henry Dashwood's. I thank Heaven that, in spite of my poverty, I have encouraged the tastes which your father implanted in me. I have endeavoured to make myself a gentleman, without neglecting those who have been the companions and sharers of my misery. I leave you for ever. I leave you to your fatal error, and return to the river and the streets; but some day, perhaps, you may remember and regret—*not* Richard Ashton, heir to Mark Ashton's wealth—but Dick the Diver, the fireside companion of old days."

The girl, as he spoke, was nearly suffocated with emotion.

" Dick, Dick—forgive me !" she cried, clasping her hands. " I knew nothing—I never dreamed—"

" Hush ! say no more," said Dick bitterly. " I will go."

As he said these words, there was a hurried step along the hall, and Henry Dashwood entered the room.

He glanced from one to the other in utter amazement.

"What means this?" he cried—"how dare you come here?"

"I came to see *you*," replied Dick the Diver, undauntedly; "but my mission, apparently, has had another ending. Consequently, I shall return at another time. I cannot speak now in the same way that I desired."

Dashwood was white with passion.

In his hand he held a large riding whip, which he slashed against his own legs as he talked.

"Why, you young whelp!" he cried, "do you dare to talk to me, as if you had the free *entrée* of my house? Be off, or I will—"

"Stay," cried Dick, "do not give way to such passion. I wish to speak to you as I have done to Miriam yonder. I have told her that I am Richard Ashton, son of Mark Ashton who, for all I know, is dead—murdered by your friend, the mate of the *Valparaiso*. What I shall ask next time is, why you kept my papers and my money. I haven't the proofs yet, but I shall in time."

Henry Dashwood literally foamed with rage.

"How dare you?" he cried, raising his whip.

But Dick stopped him with a gesture.

"Do not think we are on the river now, Mr. Dashwood," he said; "remember we are in Park-lane, in your house, where a cry of murder might bring your servants even to the rescue of a guest. Think of one thing—in me, boy as I am, you have a bitter enemy. I saw the attempted murder of the Lascar; but, worse for you, I know his secret."

Dashwood's eyes blanched, his hands clenched, and his form trembled as he listened; and he staggered beneath the last blow.

Miriam Morris eyed him in wonder, and almost shrank from Dick, as, advancing towards her as he neared the door, he spoke again—

"See," he said, "Henry Dashwood fears *me*—the boy: how will he fear the man who comes and says, 'Give me back my name, my wealth, my home."

And then, as Miriam swooned into Dashwood's arms, he quitted the room.

## CHAPTER XXV.

### THE LION-TAMER.

"OOK here, Dick—here's a go!" cried the Joyful Haddock one evening, as they were just outside Daddy Spindle's. "Here's a bill!"

As he spoke, he handed the Diver a large placard, on which were inscribed the words—

TREMENDOUS EXCITEMENT!

## FEARFUL FIGHTS IN THE ARENA!!

### OMOIO,

The Greatest Lion-Tamer in the World, has the pleasure of announcing that he will appear this Evening and during the Week at the Blue Ship Hall, and exhibit his grand troupe of

## PERFORMING LIONS.

The SCENES IN THE ARENA will be the most terrific and exciting ever witnessed.

His daughter, the Beautiful Fatima, will also exhibit her favourite Lioness ALEXANDRA, who will carry her round the arena in the character of Una.

Admission 6d.

"Oh, s'help me tater!—only a tanner!" cried the Joyful Haddock. "Will you come, Dick? It's only over the water, just by Tiger Bay."

"All right," said Dick; and they went, passing over the river as usual in their boat.

The place where the performance was to take place was a huge barn near the riverside, a tavern called the Blue Ship, whose windows overlooked the Thames.

This barn had been fitted up with some attempt at decoration in the way of garlands of flowers around the walls, and lamps and so on, and flags.

The seats were placed in a circular form round a kind of arena, with high iron railings, but no covering above.

At one end of this arena was a large cage, from which every now and then proceeded load roars which sent a thrill of horrible pleasure through the veins of the audience.

And what an audience it was.

It was a living mass of both sexes and of all ages; men of every grade, some well-dressed, others in ragged shirt sleeves, boys and girls, women with babies at their breasts, all disregarding one another, and having eyes only for the spot where the thrilling scenes were about to be enacted.

Dick the Diver and the Joyful Haddock reached the place just as Omoio entered the arena leading Fatima by the hand.

The latter attracted at first the attention of all present.

She was about sixteen years of age, dressed in a garb which has familiarized itself to English sightseers by being worn by female acrobats — viz., a tight-fitting corset of variegated stuff, red satin trunks and tights, displaying the rounded limbs far above the knees.

Her feet were encased in red leather boots,

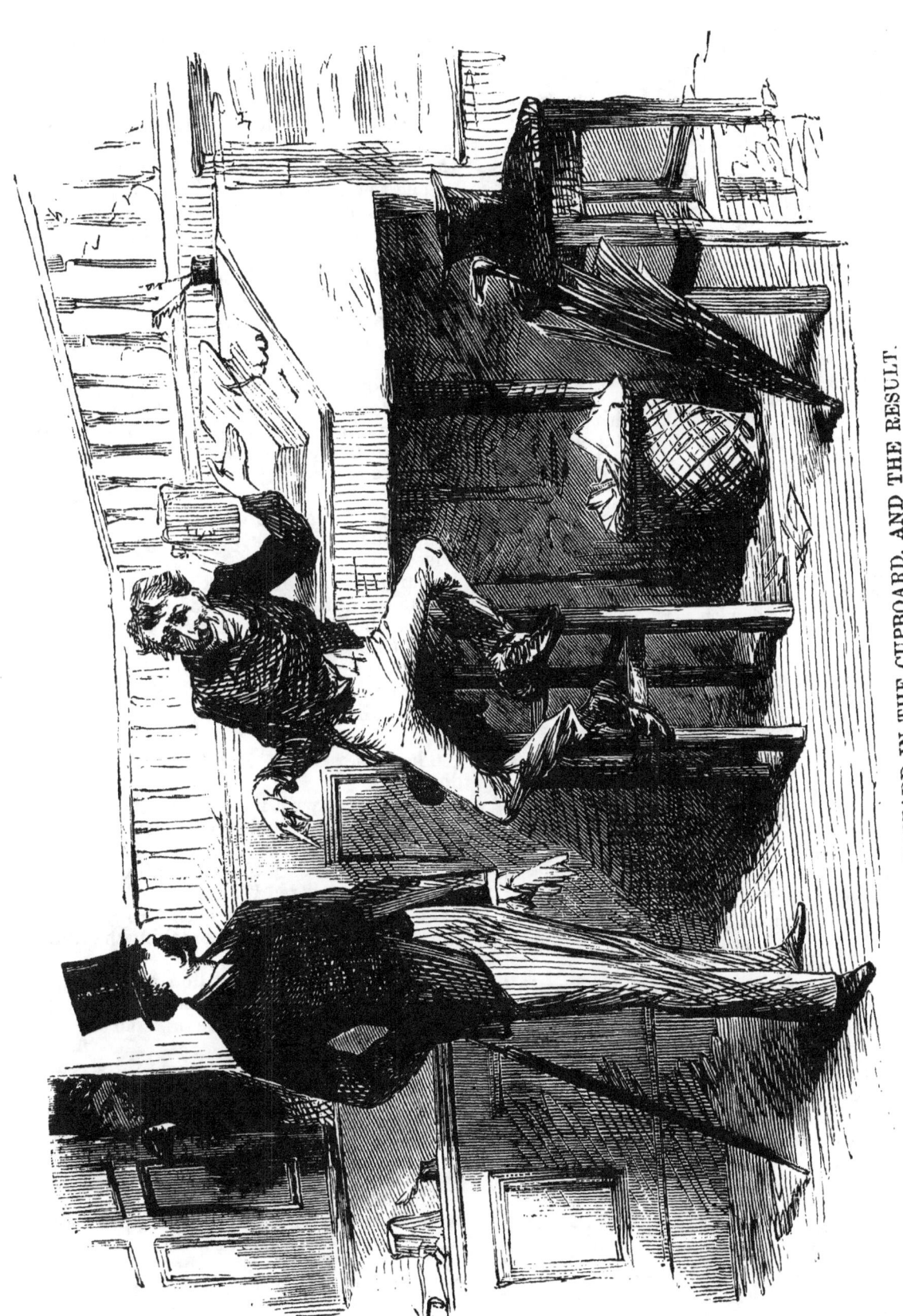

WHAT DICK HEARD IN THE CUPBOARD, AND THE RESULT.

trimmed with white fur, and a dainty little Turkish cap was on her head.

Lovely in form as well as in face, she—as I have said—attracted at first the whole notice of Dick the Diver.

But the instant his eyes fell upon the lion-tamer himself, his whole attention became riveted upon him.

Disguised he might be, but he felt certain that Omoio was no other than Hasib the Lascar.

He was dressed in the ordinary dress of performers in the circus, and his head was ornamented with some savage kind of head-gear.

But the bright eye was there—the clear-cut features, the noble mien.

He glanced round him with a proud, defiant look; and then, having taken Fatima by the hand, he bowed with her to the audience, and a cage being unfastened, a splendid lioness came bounding into the arena.

A thrill of horror and fascination passed through the veins of the audience as the splendid beast approached Fatima, who, touching its head with a wand, commanded it to kneel.

The docile creature obeyed; and then seating herself upon its back, the daring girl went the circuit of the arena, guiding the animal by a silken bridle.

A word spoken gently from her lips seemed to have power entirely to control the lioness, which, after carrying round the lovely representative of Una, the Goddess of Innocence, went through a variety of evolutions at her bidding, and then retired quietly to her cage.

Then, with a loud yell, two huge lions came bounding forth, while Fatima sprang aside and clambered to a little seat, which was specially reserved for her on the summit of the barrier.

Hasib—for Dick the Diver was certain it was he, in spite of the false name and the disguise—faced the two brutes with truly regal pride and resolute daring.

Both the beasts were fine specimens of the wild kings of the forest; but although their aspect was fierce by its very nature, they seemed at first to be so entirely under the dominion of their master, that they had no more terror for him than some domestic animal would have had.

Obedient to the will of the man who had conquered them, they went through a variety of evolutions, crouching at his feet, standing upon their hind legs, and even engaging in a mimic battle with one another.

As the eyes of the two wild creatures grew brighter and brighter in their contention, Dick began to feel a kind of nervousness pervade him.

His heart appeared oppressed by some vague presentiment of evil.

What it was he knew not.

But in spite of this ignorance of the absolute cause of his dread, he could not help watching the movements of the animals and their master with more eagerness than ever.

The performer meanwhile was quite unconscious of the terrible interest he excited.

He, in fact, was the most cool and unconcerned of all present.

He walked around the arena with calm dignity, every now and then bowing to the audience, but always contriving to keep his eyes fixed upon the fearful monarchs of the woods.

The Joyful Haddock was in ecstacies.

"Oh, my eye! aint it fine?" he kept saying, clapping his hands with delight. But in spite of digs and pokes in the ribs, Dick took no notice of him.

He could see by the anxious look of Fatima that something more than ordinary was happening, and he kept his eyes fixed with a fascinated gaze upon the tall form of the Lascar, as he strode to and fro in the arena.

The exhibition approached its climax.

Dick the Diver noticed, with a certain feeling of uneasiness, that one of the lions seemed restive and obstinate.

He observed that Hasib's play with him was not all sport.

The other noble animal was perfectly docile.

Hasib acted with more than usual energy, and drew down thunders of acclamation.

The brave fellow smiled bitterly at the thought that the public gave him applause for what endangered his life.

The brute, which had been trained to be apparently aggressive, was breaking the limits of control.

The climax came—the lion sprang upon him; but it was in sportiveness no longer, his teeth grazed through the skin and touched blood.

Then the wild instinctive thirst was aroused; and Hasib said a prayer, for he was down upon his knees.

He knew it would be a fight for life, and he tried to collect strength in nerve and muscle.

The audience were electrified. Many of them had seen the contest often, but never seen it so protracted as now.

Dick the Diver rose: he would have fought a tiger or a demon, for he knew no fear.

He saw Hasib's peril, and said—

"You are in danger."

"Not if I can get my footing," Hasib said.

And then the gallant lad leapt into the arena.

He seized the lion's shaggy mane, and struck it fearful blows with his clenched hand.

"If we live," Hasib said, "I will thank you for this.

Dick the Diver's voice rang out like a clarion.

"Let the keepers come," he said, "and bring a lighted torch. Take the lion that is quiet to his cage."

He spoke too late.

The keepers came; they were always in attendance near.

They brought a lighted torch, and Dick took it; but they could not take the other lion to his cage.

The faithful creature saw its master's danger, and what it had been taught to do in play it did in earnest now; it sprang upon its forest brother, and fought for its human master's life.

The spectators rose in a body.

None thought of going out—the terrible spectacle chained them to the spot.

Hasib's courage rose to a fiery pitch.

To be rebelled against by a creature he had trained and fed stung him to more than mortal dauntlessness.

He swung his massive club like a sledge hammer, and dealt blow after blow upon the lion's skull.

The brute cowered for a moment.

It seemed to recognize a spirit stronger than his own; and in that moment—to avert a worse catastrophe—Hasib signalled the keepers to take the docile one to its cage.

It went at its master's word.

"Now," said Hasib, grimly, to the lion, "your death or mine."

Dick the Diver was not idle.

He beat the monster with his burning brand each time it sprang at Hasib, who followed it and struck it with crushing force.

It staggered over, and unfortunately for Hasib the club fell from his hand.

He drew his revolver then.

Twice he fired, and at the second shot the lion turned from him with a roar of pain, half blind with fire from Dick the Diver's brand and its own blood.

The entire audience seemed to give one shriek, and shrank back to make a path, for the lion leaped the barrier, and as it leapt with open jaws seized Fatima in its huge mouth.

For an instant the whole of the audience stood spellbound.

Not a single soul was there who cared to

face the infuriated beast, as it stood by the closed door glaring round at the people, with the fainting girl still suspended in his jaws.

After a moment, however, two persons sprang forward to the rescue—the one Hasib the Lascar, the other Dick the Diver.

One terrific blow of his loaded whip caused the infuriated animal to drop his prey to the earth; another, and he crouched down ready for a spring.

Dick, in spite of the fearful scene, had not dropped the flaming brand; and as he saw the lion ready to dash upon his victim, he thrust the flaming torch into the animal's mouth.

Then as the animal rolled over in his agony, Dick drew his pistol from his breast and shot it through the brain.

Hasib the Lascar had up to this moment preserved his presence of mind; but now when the danger was over, his nerves gave way; and as he saw Dick raise Fatima in his arms, he fell suddenly, with a cry as of pain, upon the body of the dead lion.

---

## CHAPTER XXV.

### FATIMA.

HERE was a shout of applause from the till then frightened audience, when they saw Dick the Diver standing triumphantly over the body of the dead lion.

But Dick, though fire might have flashed from his eyes, felt anything but real triumph —that was a thought which might enter his mind afterwards; but now it was full of something very different.

Kneeling down as soon as he saw that all life was crushed out of the savage beast, he raised Fatima, the Lion Queen, in his arms and examined her limbs to see if any hurt was discernible.

But there was nothing much to be seen.

Fright seemed to have been the principal cause of her losing her senses for the time; for with the exception of one large spot of blood on the outer part of one thigh, where the animal's teeth had scratched her, she was untouched.

While Hasib was being attended to by the other persons around, Dick raised the beautiful creature in his arms, and bore her to a spot where she could obtain refreshment.

Here, some wine being administered, she opened presently her large eyes, and fixed them upon him wonderingly.

"Who are you?" she cried—though there was a glance in her brilliant orbs which spoke of a sudden interest.

"You know me not," he answered; "but I know well your father, Hasib."

She smiled.

"He is not my father," she said. "But tell me, what has happened? Where is Hasib?" and then she added, glancing at her leg, "what does this wound mean?"

"It means," said a voice beside them—a

voice slow, stern, and solemn—"it means that both you and I owe our lives to him. Come, let us leave this place; and in our own home we can explain things better."

"But the audience!" replied the girl, looking round in wonderment, "what has become of them?"

"They are satisfied," said Hasib, with a grim smile; "they have seen more than they expected."

In a few minutes, Dick, with Hasib and Fatima, still in their arena costume, entered a cab, and were driven towards a house somewhere in the vicinity of the Tower.

Here they were ushered into a suite of apartments, utterly unlike what might have been expected as the home of such persons, and in the best of these rooms Fatima was left alone with Dick, who, gazing at her in all the beauty of her picturesque dress, felt within him a strange sensation which neither Miriam nor Alice had ever excited.

It was a marvel, perhaps, that it should be so.

Miriam Morris had been his first love, Alice had created in his mind an intense interest after the first love had deceived him; but perhaps this gentle, yet bold, winning, yet resolute child of nature, as she seemed to be, had more in common with him than the others.

She bound her wound up carelessly, by placing a handkerchief tightly round her leg, as if she had been used to such catastrophes; and then, seating herself near Dick, said, with a smile—

"You are a brave lad. Did you ever face a raging lion before?"

"Never; but I would do it again in such a cause," said Dick the Diver, scarcely thinking what he said. "I saw Hasib and you in danger, and I sprang to the rescue. Tell me, who is Hasib? Why is he here? He gave me, not many days ago, a paper which he asked me to preserve two years, because he was leaving England, and should not return before the expiration of that time; and now here I find him remaining in Tiger Bay taming wild beasts."

Fatima placed her soft little hand in his.

"He has his reasons for remaining here," said Fatima, "you may depend upon that. But see, here he comes; and—oh, Heavens! the end is coming—his disguise is gone at last."

Dick the Diver heard not her words.

He himself was petrified with amazement, for the person who entered the room, though he was indeed Hasib, was not Hasib as he had known him before.

The dark skin had vanished, the black hair was a soft brown. Hasib was no longer a Lascar, but a European.

Dick sprang to his feet astonished.

"What does this mean?" he cried. "Am I dreaming, or are my senses playing me some delusive trick?"

"No, my boy," cried Hasib, taking his hand, "it is no dream; but the beginning of the end of that story which commenced for you when Mark Ashton was supposed to have been murdered on board the *Valparaiso*. Sit down there, and I will tell you a story."

Dick, scarcely knowing what he was doing, sat down by the side of Fatima; and the supposed Lascar began as follows:—

"The ship *Orizona* was on her homeward voyage to Chili, after a voyage of many months, during which time matters, with some exceptions, had gone forward quite pleasantly.

"The credit of this evidently did not belong to the captain; for he was a surly, drunken brute, and had amused himself during most of the voyage by approaching the men unseen, giving them a violent kick, striking them with his rattan, and sometimes with some heavier implement.

"But the sailors dared not resent even this treatment, and for the sake of the second mate, who was a great and deserved favourite with them, they bore it in silence.

"Among the crew there was a young man by the name of Mark Ashton, a good sailor, and a general favourite with all except the captain, who appeared to feel an especial spite against him, simply because he was a true man.

"One day, Ashton was seated below, when one of his favourites, by the name of Mark Arundel, approached him and said—

"'Well, Mark, the voyage is nearly over. By to-morrow we may expect to see land.'

"'Yes, and I thank Heaven for it.'

"'Why do you speak so earnestly, Mark?'

"'I want to leave the ship.'

"'I didn't think you were in such a hurry.'

"'But I tell you I am. I have long felt an inclination to throttle that dog; and when I saw him strike you to-day, Arundel, I could scarcely restrain myself.'

"'Oh, I don't mind that. He is a drunken beast, and not worth noticing, considering that everything goes on so pleasantly.'

"'I can't look upon it in that light. He is a prominent officer, and ought to be a gentleman. If he should strike me, I—'

"'Oh, it is not very likely he would strike you.'

"'I think it is very likely.'

"'Why so?'

"'I couldn't but frown to-day when the wretch struck you. He observed it, and although he didn't say anything at the time, I could read his intention at a glance.'

"'Suppose he should strike you, Mark?'

"'I believe I should hurl him to my feet, and place my heel upon his cowardly neck.'

"'Then you'd swing from the yard-arm.'

"'I know it.'

"'It would be hard to die for such as he.'

"'True. Well, I don't know how I should act in the case of a blow. I never yet have received a blow, and I hope I never will. I could not endure the degradation. Why, Arundel, I really believe that if I were to be flogged on shipboard it would render me a raving fiend for the remainder of my life, if it did not kill me on the spot.'

"At that moment Mark was summoned to the deck. He quickly obeyed, and set about performing the duty devolving upon him with an alacrity and cheerfulness in keeping with his character. He had glanced quickly around, and the captain was not to be seen.

"Suddenly Mark felt a violent blow upon the head. He staggered, and fell to the deck.

"But his senses did not forsake him.

"He was satisfied from whence the blow came, and looking up he saw the captain standing near him.

"For the moment Mark had not the power to move, or he would have leaped upon the captain like a tiger.

"As it was, he could not but exclaim—

"'Oh, you accursed brute! But I will be even with you.'

"This was enough.

"A guard of marines were instantly called up; and in a few seconds Mark found himself in irons, and a fast prisoner below.

"He knew his fate now—flogging.

"Boy and man, he had been a sailor for twenty years, and had never received a blow.

"But now his hour had arrived, and he must submit to that which he had always believed would be death to him.

"The night passed slowly away.

"Morning came, and the hours of day passed on.

"Towards evening the crew were startled by the dread summons of the boatswain and his mates at the principal hatchway—a summons which always sends a shudder through every manly heart in a frigate.

"'All hands to witness punishment ahoy!'

"The cry appeared harsh and unrelenting.

"It pierced every part of the ship, and not a heart but felt its dismal echo was there to be found, save he who claimed to be the master there.

"In a short time the crew had crowded around the mainmast.

"All must come.

"All wore sad faces.

"Soon the officers were arranged on one side, and the captain, taking his place among them, cried—

"'Master-at-arms, bring up the prisoner.'

"All were silent as Mark was brought on deck, guarded by marines, and placed upon the gratings.

"The captain began—

"'You, Mark Ashton, are about to be punished for using disrespectful language and threats towards your captain.

"'Have you anything to say?'

"'I have used no disrespectful language,' replied Mark, in a firm voice.

"'What!' cried the captain. 'Did you not call me an accursed brute?'

"'I did.'

"'And what language do you call that?'

"'Respectful to you.'

"'How?'

"'It is complimentary, for you are worse than a brute.'

"The captain could scarcely suppress his rage; but he did so, for he felt that his revenge was to come.

"So he asked—

"'Did you not threaten me?'

"'I do not recollect that I did.'

"'Did you not say that you would be even with me?'

"'So maddened was I by the blow you gave me, that I might have done such a thing. If I did, I repeat it now; and I swear before my Maker that I will be avenged for the first blow you gave me, and for every one I receive now.'

"'Boatswain's mates, do your duty,' yelled the captain.

"'Stop one instant,' cried Mark, calmly. Then he continued. 'Mates, I can't blame you for striking the blow, for you must let me say in advance that I forgive you for it. But to you, captain, I say once more, stop this work, or you will find it the bitterest of your life.'

"'Lay on, mate,' yelled the captain.

"'My last warning!'

"'Lay on, mate.'

"The keen scourge hissed through the air, and fell with a cutting, hissing sound upon the mark.

"Mark trembled visibly; but his teeth were set, and no sound escaped him.

"The first blow barely left a mark; but as the successive ones fell, red ridges began to appear, livid lines of bruised and mangled flesh were drawn, the muscles rose in knotted cords, and the whole of the naked back showed a livid and purple colour.

"Sixteen, seventeen, and the ridges broke, the blood streaming down upon the deck.

"Twenty, and a groan, the first, escaped Mark's lips.

"Then he cried, although the voice seemed weak—

"'Farewell, messmates, farewell!'

"Twenty-two, Mark sank, only sustained by the rope attached to his thumbs.

"Twenty-three and twenty-five—did they not fall upon the back of a corpse?

"'Cut him down,' growled the captain, as he turned away.

"The order was obeyed.

"Every one expected to see Mark fall upon the deck lifeless.

"But it was not so.

"No sooner were his hands free, than he bounded up and leaped towards the captain like a tiger.

"That officer drew his pistol as he detected the movement, but he was not quick enough. The weapon was flung aside by the frantic man, and the wretch clutched by the throat.

"Then Mark lifted him from the deck as if he had been a mere child.

"Nearly every officer rushed to the rescue of their captain; but it was of no avail. Over the bulwarks into the foaming sea went Mark and his persecutor, the enraged sailor still retaining his grip upon the throat of his foe.

"A fearful wail escaped the captain.

"Efforts were made to save him, but the blood that now floated over the surface where the two men had disappeared proclaimed all efforts useless.

"Darkness was just falling over the sea, when Mark Arundel, leaning over the bulwarks, heard a faint cry, proceeding as it were from the water; and as he leaned over to see what it meant, he saw Mark Ashton clinging to the stern chains.

"It was from this moment that they became firmer friends than ever. For in spite of the fact that Ashton was regarded by the rules of the service as nothing better than a murderer, Arundel drew him on board, and kept him secreted in the hold until they reached land.

"After this Arundel never returned to his ship, but with his bosom friend started for the gold mines.

"Here both of them succeeded in acquiring riches, both of them incited to their work by the same thoughts—thoughts of the dear ones they had left in England.

"It was just at the moment that they were about to return to England that Mark Ashton was taken seriously ill, and Arundel volunteered to come to England, and fetch his wife and family out to him.

"It was he who was murdered on board the *Valparaiso*; and as if some spirit-whisper had told him the fate of his friend, Mark Ashton was in England almost before the body of his companion was cold in the earth."

The Lascar paused a moment, and then, as if unable to restrain himself any longer,

he threw his arms around Dick the Diver, exclaiming—

"I am Mark Ashton, Richard, and you are my son!"

"And who, then, is Fatima?" asked Dick, after the first few moments of excitement were over.

"She is the daughter of my best and most unfortunate friend, Mark Arundel," said Ashton; "and I hope, if circumstances are propitious, that she will become my daughter."

Then, turning to Fatima, he said—

"Go, Helen, and take off for the last time the garb of the Lion Queen. Leave us together : we have much to say."

## CHAPTER XXVI.

### DION NIP IN A NEW CHARACTER.

HENRY DASHWOOD, by an exercise of that fatal power which he possessed over Alice Daly, contrived one night to make her accompany him in a state of unconsciousness to the chamber of his wife, whom the villain ruthlessly murdered.

Then he endeavoured to persuade the poor, horror-stricken girl that she had perpetrated the foul crime.

Feeling convinced, however, of her own innocence, she fled home in terror. But her perils were not yet over.

That very night Dion Nip broke into the house, and thinking he had obtained a great prize, bore her off in triumph to a place of secrecy.

Alice Daly's disappearance caused great consternation and alarm.

At first the father and mother were astounded by the non-appearance of their daughter; but as Mrs. Daly said that she voluntarily went with Dion Nip, they imagined that she might be absent for some time upon some private business of her own.

But as time flew by, and three days had come and gone without any intelligence being heard of, all the family, and Henry Dashwood as well, became greatly concerned.

Dashwood, as we have seen, in his character of Caleb Stringer, had resolved to make Alice his wife.

In her sane moments, as we have seen, she hated him.

But when under the influence of that fatal power which he knew so well how to exercise over her, she appeared to love him madly, fondling and caressing him as if she were the most passionate of lovers.

He had resolved, accordingly, that the

marriage should take place when she was in this condition, so that she would not even be able to observe that the name she signed on the register was not Alice Stringer, but Alice Dashwood.

Dashwood, therefore, as time went on, began to be maddened with uneasiness.

Knowing that, unless some real heir to the Ashton estates turned up, Alice was the next heiress through her father, he was furious at even the chance of losing her.

Pretending, therefore, to be solicitous for the good of the family, he offered a reward of fifty pounds for her discovery.

It was on the evening of the day on which the bills offering the reward were issued that Thomas Nip entered his curious old room by the river, where he found his son Dion seated by the fire indulging in a reverie.

"Dion!" cried his father, "there's a reward out for Daly's daughter."

"How much?" said Dion, starting.

His father eyed him narrowly.

"Fifty pounds."

Dion burst into a loud laugh.

"Why, they must be mad," he said, "to offer such a sum as that. If they'd said two thousand pounds, I could have understood it."

"Why so much?"

"She's the heiress of Ashton. Don't I know it? Haven't I heard all the story from you? Don't I know she's a prize?—that is, if any one could get hold of her."

"Just so, good boy," said Thomas Nip, with a laugh; "but the fact is, you *do* know where she is; you have got the prize; and my advice is to take the fifty pounds at once."

"Why, when she is the heiress?"

"She is not the heiress. She was; but the true heir is found."

Dion sat back in his chair aghast.

"You are jesting, father, surely," he said.

"No, this very night I have received the news that the one whom I have always believed to be the heir, is the right one."

"And who is it?"

"The poor street boy, the enemy of that villain Dashwood," said Thomas Nip. "It was I, thank Heaven, who put him on the scent of his fortune, and I hope he will reward me."

Dion sat for a time as if crushed by the blow.

He had, indeed, indulged in such strange dreams, such wild anticipations; and now everything was crumbling in the dust.

"After all, the right road's the best," thought he. "I'll have this fifty pounds, and I'll start off to another country and begin afresh. The old man's got on better by acting on the square, and I had better do the same."

"Well, look here, father," he said aloud, "if that's the case, I'd better confess that I have got the young lady, safe under lock and key. There, don't begin any of your preach-ing, dad. I have been preaching to myself, and I'm going to have a good try at reform. What I want to know is, how am I going to get the money? If I make a clear confession, they'll be doubting whether to pay me or not."

"I'll settle that, Dion," said Nip. "I'll go to them now."

The old man at once bustled off towards the house of Augustus Daly, where he found Mrs. Daly in tears, the father walking in deep agitation to and fro, and Henry Dashwood acting his part as comforter.

"Do not despair, dear madam," said Nip, as he entered. "I come to bring you excellent news. You know *me*, Mr. Stringer," he added, turning to Dashwood; "I am the head clerk to Messrs Greed and Tact, and you can trust me. If you will kindly give me notes or gold for the amount of fifty pounds, I will guarantee that Miss Daly shall be restored to you in this room within four hours."

The mother clasped her hands and uttered a cry of joy.

"Where is she, then?" she cried.

Nip smiled.

"Ah!" he said, "that I must not say. I was visited by some one to-night whose name is better known by the police than it is respected; and I only obtained your daughter's address on oath of secrecy."

"Very well," said Dashwood, "let us have no delay; here are the notes."

Nip took them, crushed them methodically, and said—

"Perfectly correct. Remain up, and before the four hours are up, Miss Daly shall be in this room untouched and happy."

When Thomas Nip—rattling up to the door in a Hansom cab—reached home, he found Dion pacing to and fro in a state of intense agitation, but dressed in his best, and looking the handsome fellow he really was.

There was a change in his manner as well as in his dress; and as his father came in he caught him by the shoulder.

"Father," he said, "am I a gentleman by birth? I know you educated me well, and so on, and I've been a blackguard and thrown away all my advantages; but if I thought—"

"Think, then, Dion," said old Nip, smiling. "You know that some time ago I was convicted of a crime, and punished; but I was innocent, as I can swear before Heaven. My name is *not* Nip, but Wentworth, and I was the son of a colonel in the army."

"Good!" said Dion, firmly. "I'll go now and fetch Alice."

When he reached the house, the doctor received him with a scared look.

"Your patient has been telling me a strange

story," he said.    She is either mad, or she has the life of a man upon her lips."

A shudder passed through the frame of Dion Wentworth.

"Let me see her at once," he said.

He found her sitting at the window, gazing out upon the starlit night.  No light in the room but that of the moon, which streamed in a silver halo over her form.

Dion went to her, and took her hand.

"I am come to take you home," he said. And then kneeling at her feet, he added— "And I come also to crave your forgiveness. You are perfectly free, but I entreat you to tell me the story which you repeated to the doctor."

Alice was in no mood to tell anything while bars surrounded her.  Nor did she pause to blame Dion for the part he had had in her abduction; for her foolish fancies having passed, she felt no longer under the influence of Dashwood; so pressing his hand warmly, she bade him rise, adding—

"We will talk on my way home.  I have a terrible story to tell; which will, I hope, be the means of bringing the guilty to justice."

The old doctor was paid liberally, and the two were soon rushing along towards home.

Here Alice told the hideous story of the murder of Mrs. Dashwood, in which she played so astounding a part; and after hearing it, Dion said gently—

"Miss Daly, your father and mother are unaware that I have had anything to do with your abduction; pray allow them to remain in ignorance, and, meanwhile, I will tell you a secret.  The man whom you believe to be Caleb Stringer is no other than Henry Dashwood, husband of the unfortunate woman who believed herself to be the widow, but was really the wife, of Mark Ashton."

"Who is also dead."

"No; who lives to declare his son, Richard Ashton, hitherto known as the street boy, Dick the Diver, the heir to Ashton Meads!"

Before proceeding to 17, Park-lane, Dion called at Scotland-yard; and when he en-

tered the house two detectives entered with him.

He went boldly into the room where Mrs. Daly, her husband, Nip, and Henry Dashwood were assembled.

"I bring you back your daughter, Mrs. Daly," said Dion; "and I bring you news also of your pretended friend, Caleb Stringer. His name is really Henry Dashwood, and he is the murderer of the wife of Mark Ashton.  Constables, take your prisoner."

But Henry Dashwood was too quick for them.

With one wild look of desperation round the room, he dashed towards a window, and, flinging it open, sprang out into the street below before any one could attempt to prevent him.

The wretched man had not even a hope of safety; and when discovered, was lying a crushed and mangled mass upon the pavement.

Our story is soon told.

The papers which Thomas Nip had in his possession, together with the testimony of Mark Ashton himself, soon established the identity of Dick the Diver, who had been delivered over to Daddy Spindle at the time when the friends of Mark Ashton had supposed him to be murdered and out of the way.

Miriam Morris married, after a time, the young baronet who had been introduced to her by Henry Dashwood, but lived an unhappy and uneventful life; while Dion Wentworth became, after a while, the husband of Alice Daly.

Daddy Spindle, Bully Wrench, and the Joyful Haddock all now fade out of our history; but the latter, who has now a shop of his own, and is a flourishing tradesman, still talks of the hundred pounds he received on the day of the marriage of Dick the Diver with the beautiful daughter of the murdered traveller of the *Valparaiso*.

THE END.